A Labyrinth in Red

Timeus & Hemanth

Made with ♥ on the Notion Press Platform
www.notionpress.com

CONTENTS

Author – Timeus

PREFACE

Normal life filled with insignificant events dramatized by simple storytelling tools. That is a way to describe this collection of short stories. The world is filled with an abundance of stories with only a few lucky enough to write and convey these stories. When we listen and observe our day-to-day lives and our surroundings, we can find these. These passionate, raw, unadulterated tales of life around us. It is humbling to be a part of something so significant, this rich tapestry of stories. I am merely using this medium to share some of these real ideas around us that appeal to something deeply human within us.

They are a personal insight into life from my point of view, a 20 year old college student living in Chennai with the dramatization of normal events in life. They are mostly fictional but grounded in some real life observations. They offer more than what is superficially seen with every story having a more complex idea with the social background and societal issues that we face today. The reader is free to interpret the ideas for themselves and perhaps ponder upon the issues they find.

These stories are meant to stir something within all of us, some emotion that makes us think about something greater than ourselves. I do not wish to over philosophize the ideas I have presented but leave the reader to do that themselves. The stories each have a philosophy behind them that the reader is free to interpret. These stories are the first that I have published and so I hope they have an impact on the reader in some way as that is the wish of any writer, to leave the reader with something to think about. They are all experimental in a way and I hope reading this brings something new in your mind and affects you in some way or the other.

for the people who try

SCARLET

"Memory is a wonderful thing if you don't have to deal with the past"

– Richard Linklater

I

THE CRIMSON CAR

#1

There it was. In all its glory. My vessel to take me to Olympus. A dusty, red Volkswagen Polo stood outside my house with an L board. It was standing right there, waiting for me. I slowly made my way to the car already imagining myself with a license, driving to college, and showing off the fact that I could drive. Ah, what adoration I would receive! I'd drive everyone everywhere and go wherever I wanted whenever I wanted. Need a ride? Better Call Christian. Well, doesn't have a great ring to it but we can work on that. I opened the door to the car that would change my life. All that was left to do was to learn how to drive.

I sat in the driver's seat and adjusted the position till I felt comfortable. I knew the basics I suppose. Slowly release the clutch while slowly pressing the accelerator. Simple enough. Right foot – accelerator and brake, left foot – clutch. Hands at ten and two on the steering wheel or nine and three. Nothing complicated. Honestly don't get all the fuss. This was going to be easy enough. Just had to wait for my driving instructor to arrive so I could "wow" him. I could see him already so impressed how a first-time driver like myself was such a natural. Max Verstappen, move aside.

On cue, entered my Driving Instructor, a bald guy probably in his late 50s with empty eyes, a desolate face, and a pot belly. This looked promising. He brought another student with him, a woman in her late 20s perhaps, who sat behind. I paid no attention to her as I was locked in. This was it. It was my moment. My time to shine. Nothing could stop me. I turned on the music which began to play Eminem's Lose Yourself as I hyped myself up. The instructor turned off the music as abruptly as I had started it but I didn't let that stop me as I played it in my head.

"Drive," instructed my Driving Instructor. This was it. I was Ryan Gosling himself. I was about to do it. I pressed the clutch as hard as I could, and I turned the ignition. The car came to life. Slowly... I put it into first, released the clutch as gently as I could. I would not let it stall. There would be no stalling. Not today. The car began to wobble ever so slightly and I gave it a little throttle... It began to move! Yes! It was moving! We're doing it. The car was mobile. Houston, we have lift-off! I gave it a little more throttle in my excited state and... The engine cut off! NOOOOOOOOOOOOOOOOOO!!!! I had committed the cardinal sin! IT WAS MOVING! HOW HAD I STALLED?!

I hung my head in shame and slowly turned to face my Driving Instructor. He was unmoved. He stared ahead as if he still expected me to drive.

"Go," he said without even looking at me. I had another chance? Okay, then. This was it. I was going to do it. I started it again and put it into gear. THIS WAS IT! I was going to make it. I slowly released the clutch just like before, this time giving more throttle and feeling it rev a little but I maintained my composure. The car shook slowly and nudged forward. I let go of the clutch almost entirely now as the car began to pick up more speed. I had done it!!! I was driving. I hit 20kmp/h. I hit the clutch again and shifted to second!

My God! This was so easy. I picked up more speed and then noticed the traffic. AHHHHHH!!!! I hit the brakes a good 20 feet behind the nearest car. The car switched off. Noooooooo. What had I done wrong this time? This was embarrassing. ARGHHH!!!

"Be mindful of your surroundings", my Driving Instructor suggested helpfully.

Sitting in that car, facing my future all I could think of was my past. The world was rushing past me. I was running out of time. I needed to drive. The growing thoughts in my head reminded me more and more of the time I was losing. I needed to drive. I had to drive. It would all be better if I could drive.

I froze amid traffic, paralyzed by doubt.

#2

I felt a strong emotion wash over me, that pleasant feeling when I revisited my hometown. The feeling that I had as a teenager with the world in front of me, a feeling I never stopped to appreciate. One might say I could still sit down and acknowledge that fact since I was just 22. The greenery, the blue skies, the warm beaches, the empty roads in the afternoon, the deserted grocery store, the house I grew up in, the friends I had, the time I had... A world of opportunity was all that lay ahead, my mind up in the clouds, filled with ambition. The difference five years can make in your life.

I met my friend at a café by the beach, a beach devoid of people. Just the clear blue skies and the sound of the waves that accompanied us. The café had a few tables occupied but I was busy being entranced by the warmth I felt in this place. What was life after the age of 20 if not a desperate attempt to trigger any form of nostalgia to remind yourselves of only the good parts of your life.

I looked at my friend, his eyes fixed on the sunset, staring ahead blissfully, unafraid of what lay ahead.

"Driving is harder than it seems, it may take me a little longer than I had anticipated." I told him following his gaze, trying to see what was so mesmerizing about what lay ahead.

He took a beat then we looked at each other.

He smiled saying, "As all things do."

"I know. There's just so much to do."

"And so little time."

"Yeah."

"You ever find yourself in Time Purgatory? You know when you're--"

"Stuck in the future but drawn into the past by some memory seeking comfort but only finding pain and now you can't go back to the future nor can you live in the present."

"Yeah..."

"Never happened to me"

"It's a funny thing, no."

"What is?"

"Ambition." He paused to look at the horizon again and continued saying, "A common misconception has ambitious people living in the future, but truc ambition lies with the people who live with those conscious enough to stay in the present while being just aware enough of what should await them."

"Is this *the* year?"

"Every year is *the* year for you," he chuckles. "You seem to miss my point. Maybe you still have time, maybe it's too late. That is for you to decide."

I sighed and began to observe my surroundings; there was a man sitting by himself reading a book and sipping coffee, a young couple lost in each other's eyes, a middle-aged happy couple with two well-behaved children as well as an unhappy couple with three misbehaving children, an old man sitting by himself staring at his beer with no one else and then there was us.

"Perhaps it is too late."

"You know the funny thing about being self-conscious. It makes us reach a state of such self-awareness that we know exactly what to do and how to do it and when to do it and yet seem so clueless and unmotivated. It's a fine line. On one hand, you need to it to become a better person but too much of it and you may never move from one place to another..."

He waits expectantly.

"Like driving a car."

I took one more look at the people in the café and woke up in my bed. I looked at the time. It was 6 AM. A new day. A new time. The past was behind, my future ahead but all I had now was the present.

II

RAHUL AND MARIA

23rd January
2:03p.m.

What could I do? Life was but a meaningless circle. I spent atleast an hour staring at the ceiling fan spinning.... round and round.... round and round.... round and round.... round and round.... round and round. Living was futile. I should talk to her again, and see where I stand, or not. No. Maybe. No, bad idea. Was there a plan? I needed a plan. A game plan. Game. I needed to game.

Yeah, we need to lock in. Got to go game. Wait, no.

What was I doing? Plans, yes. Strategy. That's how people win at anything. Football, cricket, always gotta have a plan. Skill and talent help but are useless without good tactics. Plans, strategy, tactics so important in sport, life. Should write an essay on these things. I should eat. Forget about her. Who cares

There is no her. She doesn't even care if I exist or not.

so what we talk every day and have such fun conversations and chemistry?

she sits next to me every day for no reason. obviously.

It all means nothing.

It's all just misdirection.

she's just tricking me. If I decide to make a move on her. BAM! cancelled! arrested for harassment, and life in jail. I'm the bad guy, she was just 'being nice". I "misread" all the signals. It was all just a giant conspiracy to have me jailed for life. They're all after me. ~~ARGHHHHHHH~~ !!

why is she still in my head? I need to make a new plan. I just need to figure out a way to make her like me without realizing it.

what, NO! she does like me. Doesn't she? NO, she doesn't

I'm delusional. yes, that makes more sense.

I'm just losing my mind. Delusion is our best friend. I love it. I need nothing. I want no one.

she probably doesn't even know my name. who even cares? let her die. I couldn't care less.

****

"Did I not make it obvious enough?" I said to myself as I lay on the bed staring at the ceiling fan spin round and round. "How thick-headed can guys even be? I'm trying to communicate here but it's like talking to dry cement. Try emoting once in a while why don't you? Do you understand what it means to show emotion? Does he hate me? Did I even do anything to you? What's his problem? I just want to talk. I clearly gave him all the signals. Does he think I friend-zoned him? Why would he think that? How dumb can an individual be? He is certainly pushing the boundaries of dumbness. I don't need him. I don't need any man. They're all dumb. Absolutely useless."

In walks Jane, my best friend and roommate. "What did he do this time, Maria? You've been whining nonstop." I give her a disgusted look and reply sarcastically, "I'm sorry, am I disturbing your perfect life with my sadness?" I then proceeded to bury my head in a pillow and wail.

"I'll order us some doughnuts then," she says coyly. I popped my head up briefly, "Thank you," with the most adorable smile I could conjure up, and proceeded to bury my head back into the pillow and screamed in agony.

"So what did you do?" She asked me blankly. "Nothing," I muffled incoherently into my pillow. She pushed me over and looked me in the eye. Jane was the type of girl you'd aspire to be. She was calm, confident, with luscious black hair and grey eyes. She seemed to bring out the best of everyone she met yet never the best out of herself.

Me, on the other hand, well I was quite the mess. I was not the IT girl Jane was, I had no desirable features, just some long hair which I tried my best to maintain, an okay face with no skincare routine, and to go with all this, a timid personality and nerdy glasses. Flirting with boys was most definitely not my strong suit.

Hypnotized by Jane's inquisitive gaze, I started saying, "How do men even work? Like, you know, what even makes them function? What motivates them? What are their little nuances? Do they even have nuances Lord knows, Rahul is the dumbest, stupidest guy to ever exist."

Jane smiles at me with those beautiful, white sparkling teeth reminding me of the fact that I had to wear braces for years to have mediocre teeth.

"What?" I grumbled at her with no spite whatsoever.

She just grinned back, "You really like this guy, don't you?"

I rolled my eyes in frustration, "I'm sorry, what now? Where in the entire rant did you figure that I liked this guy?"

She just up and walked away, that grin glued on her face leaving me there dumbfounded. "OH, you're just going to leave me now, aren't you? FINE, GO! I'm fine by myself. Just be like that. I'm totally fine! I don't need you or your doughnuts."

"*Like* the guy, pfft," I muttered to myself. "I am fond of him maybe. Do I like him? Maybe. But I don't need all that hassle. What do I need? Nothing. I don't want anything." I face-planted into my pillow again. *Ting!* The notification sound rang out. I grabbed it immediately to see a message from Rahul. "Sent a reel," I groaned to myself. "Wonderful, very helpful. Do I look like I want to "*see a reel*" ? What is his problem? UGHHHH!!!" I went back to the sweet embrace of my pillow.

On cue, entered Jane, "Are we feeling better now?" she said as she brought me double chocolate doughnuts. I looked up in delight, immersing myself in the smell. "Very much so," I replied joyously. We began munching on the delicious doughnuts and I updated her on the "*reel sent*". She innocently suggested we take a look.

"Well, it's just been five minutes," I said, "we can't reply." She grabbed the phone from me, "Who said anything about replying?" she said with her mouth half full and a glint in her eye.

I watched her in anxiety regretting ever adding her fingerprint to my phone as she slipped into my DM's and clicked on Rahul. I leaned in to see what the reel was about. It was one of those funny doggy videos which was dubbed over by a human voice. I started giggling, justifiably so since it was quite hilarious. Jane was unimpressed. "I should react to it, put a laughing emoji," I told Jane who remained unmoved. "Ummmm, Jane...," I said shakily. She got up and said, "Maybe you shouldn't. Make him work for it, you know. It's just a reel. Let him put in some effort." I laughed nervously, "Surely, you cannot be serious." My smile faded as she looked back mischievously.

I cautiously watched her defiant eyes with unease. "Jane, don't do this. I can't let you do this." She just smiled back smugly, "Try me." I dived at her with no real plan or balance, falling face-first onto the floor as she casually stepped back and watched me crash miserably. I cried out in pain as I rubbed my throbbing head. "Janeee –"

"I'm going to admire the sky. You should get some rest."

"Jane, wait," I said groggily getting up from the floor. She ignored me, closed the door, and clicked the lock. "AHHHHHH," I wailed as I collapsed by the door and banged on it. You choose to live in a hostel with a bunch of other people, in a so-called "community" and no one could care enough to open the door when you need them to. This was going incredibly well so far.

I don't want a relationship, who am I kidding? There's no point. What's the point? I'll just wait till I'm 30 and hope someone agrees to marry me. Yes, that will work. Most definitely. Glad we got that sorted out.

****

23rd January

7:13 p.m.

I sent her a reel. A hilarious reel. Currently waiting. Maybe she'll reply immediatly and I can use that to start a conversation. Figure something out from there then. Yes, genius. No bad feelings about this whatsoever. I should definitely do it. All I think are memes so I send memes.

WHAT HAVE I DONE? Was that too forward? No. It's just a funny meme. She probably wont see it till later. Maybe tomorrow. Who even knows? Who even cares?! I certainly dont care. Yeah, who cares. Like, why would I care! There's nothing to care about. Nothing is real. No one matters, I'm good. It's all good.

AVEEE MARIAAAAAAAAAAAAAA !!!!!!!

We're so weird. Mate, you're weird. Dammit why do we keep doing this third-person thingy, that's weird.

AHHHAHHHMMMAAAAAAA

Did I have food? I don't know.
What is food? why food! Nutrition.
No one needs nutrition anyway.
what did I want again?
Ah yes the sweet embrace of death.
It beckons me.
Death, she is beautiful. Food, yes.
Got to go get me the calories. Perhaps I would
think more clearly then. what did I have?
Fridge, nothing. wonderful. perks of living with
your family.
I have been nutritionised and ready to check my
phone. Nothing. oh, well. She probably hasn't
seen it.

****

It was becoming late. Where was she? I began to play out the scenarios in my head. Was this it? He would see I left him on seen and then block me, never speak to me again. Yes, that's what would happen. Or maybe he won't even care enough. Perhaps he'll start leaving me on seen and then where does that take us? This was turning out to be a wonderful day.

Finally, after I had lost all hope I heard the door open, and in walked Jane nonchalantly like nothing had happened. "Why are you on the floor?" She asked coyly. I was not in the mood so I just stared back dryly. "Where is my phone?" I asked as nicely as I could with no expression on my face.

"Sheesh—contemptuous much? You'll thank me. Trust me." She said with utter confidence in every word. I continued glaring at her and she rolled her eyes. "Fine, here." She handed me the phone.

I quickly unlocked it and went to see what happened but as expected, nothing. "Would I ever sabotage you?" Jane said very unhelpfully.

I began to run the scenarios in my head. Was this it? No, it couldn't be. Maybe I should reply now. Yes. No. It's probably fine. Yeah. Forget about it. No one cares. Yeah, it's all good.

It was late. I could get 4 hours of decent sleep if I went to bed right now. I set my phone down beside me and plugged into the charger. Time to sleep... eventually...

I lay there for a while. Wonder why. Just tossing around while Jane snored happily in her bed. At last, sweet exhaustion came for me to ensure I got some rest.

Or so I thought. I had one of those dreams which are super immersive, that feels like they last a long time but you actually just slept 2 hours. And it was not a nice dream. Not only did I wake up tired but also haunted by some deep feeling or memory from my dream. All I could remember were fragments. I was older, I think. Much older. I had my own house. An apartment. A job. It was all good. I felt content. Did I? It felt nice. I was independent. But there was something off. I remember sitting at my imaginary apartment, just feeling... feeling that pure, raw, devastating, heart-wrenching loneliness. It was scary. I figure we're all afraid of being alone but that emptiness, the abyss, it stared back. I had never felt it like that before. It brought something out that I never knew was inside. It was agonizing but also... warm? It was the strangest thing. As endless as it had felt, that moment in agony, there seemed to be some warmth from somewhere. A glint of light. Hope.

I had all this inside me as I made my way to class, knowing who I would run into. I could not say what I would do or what he would do. What could even happen? I made it to the hallway where my classroom was and I saw him standing there outside class by himself. I stopped short. We made eye contact. He smiled slightly and waved ever so subtly. I returned a smile and walked towards him.

III

MIDDLE CLASS

Once upon a time in a world much like yours, in fact exactly the same as yours lived a boy.
He was born on a normal day with all ten fingers and all ten toes, a healthy baby.
A bad heart the doctor said, but nothing serious he assured.
They never thought of it much.
He lived in a nice city in a nice neighbourhood.
He had a mother and a father and a brother.
His mother and father used to fight and like any marriage they were unhappy.
The boy was like any child, quite observant of these things.
He saw but never spoke, he knew he wasn't to speak.
His place was to watch, to observe.
When the boy was five, his mother left him.
He was meant to feel happy about this as his father had told him.
The boy recalled his observations and concurred.
This was a good thing, he was not to complain.
Don't speak, just observe.

They moved to a smaller town and a nice neighbourhood.
This was his new home now.
He went to his new school where he knew no one.
But no one bullied him so he was not to complain.
The other kids never said anything to him.
So he was not to complain.
He was not to listen to them when they were talking about him.
He was never to complain.
He used to come back home, joyous.
Sometimes he found his father.
Other times, he found someone else who looked like his father and was his father but spoke like someone else.
This confused him.
But he was not to complain.

This man seemed like a stranger at times but then did nice things.
He was not to complain.
The time went by and the boy was growing.
As he grew he learnt of more things.
He learnt that alcohol made his father do things.
But he also learnt of other fathers who did worse.
So he was not to complain.
He came back home every day in dread.
But he was not to complain.
The boy began to lose hope, he then got a dog.
He was not to complain.

Day and night, he cared for the dog.
But the dog always loved his father.
He was not to complain.

The boy grew older and perhaps wiser.
He realized he made mistakes he never got to correct.
He had to stop whining and be a man.
Everybody had problems much worse than him.
He was not to complain.
He entered his last years of school, an adult.
The older he grew, the more closed off he became.
This was because he was an introvert, he always was.
Except when he was a child, when he couldn't stop talking but everyone wished him to shut up.
Now everyone wished him to speak but he could never find the words.
He was not to complain.
He had a crush in school like everyone else.
He never knew whether he was in love.
And he never would.
He decided he could never afford to have a crush, that was a luxury.
He was not to complain.

He made it to 18.
He longed to leave his house, to be himself maybe.
He didn't know himself. His bad heart throbbed.
He could not leave.
Perhaps it was the dog as he said or perhaps it was fear.
Fear that he'd be no better by himself and then have nothing to blame.
He was not to complain.
He thought himself wiser now, perhaps the same things would not affect him.

He was wrong. When his father's alter ego was revealed, the boy in him would reappear no matter what he tried.

But still, it could always be worse.

He would never need for anything but he always wanted.

He could afford simple luxuries but could never ask for money.

He was not to complain.

He lived more and more in fear of tomorrow, fear that he would be reduced to what he always thought he would find, mediocrity.

He never believed in his potential, what potential?

He was good at many things but never the best so what was the point.

He was interested in many things and was passionate of few.

He could speak for hours on his passions but what was the point.

He was never good enough to himself.

He was not to complain.

He took the safe route, afraid he would fail at that even.

He wanted to be so much more, he wanted to do so much more.

He tried many times but never got past his mental block.

He did not want to wallow in self pity but wallow he did.

He was not to complain.

He went through years of college without a love interest.
He feared he lost his ability to love or perhaps never found it in the first place.
He thought himself different, perhaps it was an emotion he was never meant to feel.
He knew of many people who have gone their entire lives without true love.
He was not to complain.
Soon, the day finally came when he could leave his house.
He found a job, a stable income.
He thought day and night of "what-ifs".
He thought of all the things he missed out on.
He never truly experienced college.
He never truly experienced school.
He was never truly a part of collective, a group.
He could never belong.
He was not to complain.

All his life he was ordered to be a Christian.
"You are a Christian," his father said to him many times as a child.
What did that mean? He always thought to himself.
He never spoke out his questions in church, when he did they never answered.
He could not even belong there.
He was not to complain.
As an adult, his faith grew but never enough.
He did not find as much comfort in faith as most people did.

He believed that at the end of the day, God can only do so much for you, he had to make the important choices, the big decisions.
He could never let God do that, what was the point of that?
He was not to complain.

He grew older and would never love.
He never got a dog again.
He started to realize he had become his father and this scared him.
He could never marry because he knew what he would become.
He wanted to end the cycle.
He drank his problems away and took comfort in the fact that he was alone, at least his drinking would never hurt anyone.
His bad heart grew worse.
He could never move on to the future.
He was always stuck in the past.
In the past, he was stuck in the future.
This thought had amused him.

He realized he messed up every step of the way and perhaps there were only a few key decisions in his entire life that may have changed it entirely.
He grew to forty with no one to care for. He never went to his father's funeral.
He never spoke to his brother.
He could not go to his job any longer.
He was surprised he lived this long.

The hair on his head was almost gone.
Perhaps it was time, he thought.
He had made up his mind.
This was the end of his story.
He was not to complain.

IV

FORGIVE AND FORGET

#1

It was a routine, it happened almost every night. I didn't know what else I could do. Every decision I made from then on was always the wrong one.

"Good night, boys", I told Christian and Jacob, my two little boys aged 7 and 4. They were buried under a blanket together half asleep already. I stood there a moment just watching them and turned off the light. I closed the door to their room and made my way to the hall where the clock read 9:25. *Where was he?* Perhaps I should have been used to this by now. I could not do much, I had chosen this life for myself. I sat on the sofa while the TV ran, just waiting. The clock kept ticking. Finally, around 11 he stumbled in. The apple of my eye, my darling husband, Paul. The stench of alcohol had drifted in long before he even opened the door.

He ignored me, eyes barely open as he trudged into the bathroom and began urinating without bothering to close the door. I waited patiently. He finally made his way out and looked at me. His eyes tried to process my presence and he grinned. "Well, hello there Mizz Gorgeous." He walked over towards me and made it to the sofa only to collapse and fall asleep, his body a contortion of legs on the floor, arms to one side and the head facing the other. I slowly rearranged his body parts and put a blanket over him. "Not today, then," I muttered to myself as I saw myself to bed.

I woke up early as usual to make the kids' lunch and found him still snoring joyfully without the blanket to keep him decent. I covered him up again and got back to work. The morning went about like every other morning as I got the kids ready and took them to the bus stop. All the while, Paul snored on the sofa.

When he finally woke up, I had no energy to speak to him and he seemed to feel the same. He went about his routine as he got ready to go back to the office all without a word said. I sat alone at home weighing my options. I began my house chores unconsciously still deep in thought. I was always indecisive and perhaps that was why I even found myself in this predicament. Finding myself at a crossroads, paralysed by every choice that lay in front of me.

Before I knew it, evening had come and I had to go pick up the children from the bus stop. We had to attend a memorial that evening at our church so I got the kids ready despite their protestations while I waited for Paul to return. *He must have forgot*ten.

As usual. The entire church must be convinced that we aren't together anymore. I called Irene, my church friend who came over to pick us up with her husband, Jonathan. She did not judge us but I'm sure her husband most certainly did. I could see it in his eyes as he drove us in silence and Irene tried her best to make conversation. His eyes. On that rearview mirror. Just staring. *What was he looking at?* He smiled at me through the mirror, his wife kept raving on. *The audacity.* We made it to church and I took the kids with me to the second to last pew.

They managed to behave for the entirety of the service which was pleasing but the looks and the constant whispering of the other members began to aggravate me. It was one thing to do that after church but we were here to remember one of our own beloved member who had passed away just last year and all they could do was *gossip*.

Regardless, I decided this would never bother me and tried to focus on myself. After the service ended, I spoke with the pastor for a while and had Irene and Jonathan drop me off at home. Jonathan was still giving me the looks through the rearview mirror but I barely gave it a thought this time as my mind was processing what I would do when I went home.

We reached home by 8:30 and I made some dinner for the kids and put them to bed, closing their bedroom door. I waited by the sofa again. I thought about eating but couldn't find my appetite. The hours went by and by 1 AM I heard him pull up in the car. It was undeniably impressive how he managed to drive home drunk every night. One of the benefits of living in the small city of Pondicherry I suppose; is less traffic and more alcohol.

His breath preceded him as he made his way up the stairs and knocked on the door. I opened it as he stumbled inside straight to the bathroom. I waited on the sofa as he came out more conscious than when he went in.

A routine, I told myself that night as well.

“Heyyy...”, he slurred out. “Babby gorlll”, he began grinning and chuckling to himself.

I waited, another one of my faults as he began to rummage through the fridge looking for something.

“Where my children at?” he danced his way to the bedroom. “HELOOOOOO, LITTLE BOYSSSS, YOUR DADA ISSS HEREEEEEEE!!!

My heart started to race a little as I made my way to him to try and bring him back. I didn’t dare tell him to quiet down cause that never ended well. I slowly took his arm but he shoved me away holding his hand in front of him in a defensive position.

“STAY BACK, VILE DEMONNNN!! MY CHILDRENNNNNN!!! LITTLE BOYYSSSSS!!” he continued screaming and began to bang on the door.

Unable to control myself now, I cried out, “Paul, please!” He stopped. He looked at me intently and began to hold me by my shoulders.

“Where are my children, darling?”

I said nothing. I couldn’t bring myself to open my mouth, my voice would not work. I wanted to say something, anything but I couldn’t.

The door nudged open and out came Christian and Jacob, half asleep curious to know what woke them up. They saw their daddy and immediately became fully conscious and grew excited. He let me go and began to pat their heads as they hugged him. I watched tentatively, unsure as usual. What could I do?

"Hello, boysss. How is the school? Great, g-good. F-Future doctors and engineers, yes? GG-ood boysssss. Yeeessss. V-Very good boyssss." He stammered out.

"Okay, then, I think that's enough for now, they probably should get some sleep." I tried to interrupt.

Not a good idea. I could already see it happen. There was nothing I could do. I had aggravated him. But, no. It didn't matter, he would always be aggravated regardless of what I did. Still, I must have some accountability here, I knew this man through and through and I knew nothing good could come out of saying what I said but I said it anyway.

In his misguided anger and state of inebriation, unaware of his surroundings, he pushed away Christian who seemed to understand to stay back but Jacob persisted, holding his leg tight. Paul forcefully grabbed him off and tossed him behind, quite literally and he hit his head on that little sharp bump where the walls meet the tiles and began wailing in agony.

At this sound of pure pain, all of us froze, Paul, me, and Christian. Paul crumbled to the floor and began weeping. I tried to breathe. I could not. Nevertheless, I made my way to see what damage had been done to Jacob. His head was bleeding profusely and I grabbed him up and carried him away while guiding Christian with my other hand.

#2

At the hospital, me, Christian, Irene and Jonathan waited uneasily. My head was racing, I had nothing left in me. I was constantly praying the whole time barely acknowledging what was being said to me by Irene or anyone else. I was praying and praying, for anything, everything, but mostly for right now. I just needed Jacob to be fine then I could figure everything out which I knew was not true in the slightest but all I could do was ask for guidance. God could not make my decisions for me nor could he force me to do anything even if it was good for me, the best he could do was present me with the right opportunity and it was up to me to listen to his voice and take it. Knowing this almost all my life, all I did was make the wrong choice at every given opportunity and now I found myself here, in the hospital with my baby boy getting stitches on his head.

Irene tried to advise me on leaving Paul saying that we were always welcome to stay with them for a while but I was too preoccupied and did not say anything.

Finally, the doctor came out and brought Jacob, who had to get three stitches on his head but was so brave, that he barely gave them any trouble. He was still crying but I gently held him while the doctor gave a bunch of instructions on what to do and what not to do.

Irene offered to take us back to her house and I realized I was faced with another defining moment at a crossroads. All those prayers and God brought me back my child, safe and sound. Now he was giving me a choice. I could go to Irene's with the kids and officially begin the separation process that would ultimately lead to divorce or I could go back to *my* home and tell this man to either get better or get out. I was meant to give him one last chance. After this simple contemplation, it was my turn to finally be decisive. I had Irene and Jonathan drop me at home despite their numerous protestations.

#3

What transpired in the next few months was something I couldn't fathom and was all God's doing. That day after he had sobered up and realized what he did he tried to beg my forgiveness and I presented him with the ultimatum; either leave us or leave alcohol. He promised to never drink again and become a good father and great husband which I was very skeptical of, but since this was what God wanted me to do, I did it and watched. I did not interfere in his interactions with the kids who still absolutely adored him despite everything. I kept an eye on his progress as he suddenly began to do more work around the house, help the kids with their homework, and try to fix his relationship with me. The months went by and he only kept improving. I was astounded if I'm being honest. As much faith I had in God, this was maybe the first time I was witnessing something so amazing happening to me right in front of my eyes.

The routine was different... Nothing could go wrong now.

He even came with us to church, began to become more involved with the committees and contributed to its well-being, socializing with everyone trying to make amends. While a lot of them still judged him for his past, he did not seem to mind even saying he deserved it. *Who was this man?* It had been so long since we were first married, that I completely forgot how good he could be.

Irene began to praise me for having the strength to forgive him and was so impressed by his change she seemed to forget what he was. *I should be happy.* That's what I kept telling myself over and over as I watched this man shake his demons, accept responsibility for his actions, and become a great father and good husband. He still had small lapses every now and then when he would lose his temper but would never harm anyone else even during then always making up for it with a plethora of apologies. I had made the right choice. Yes? I trusted God and he delivered. He gave me what I wanted. The husband I married and the perfect father to my beautiful children.

How? How did he do it? How dare he get all the love and affection from my children after all that he's done? No, I couldn't think that. He deserved it. He was still their father. Yet I still couldn't rediscover my love for him.

It was 8 pm and we were all watching TV and eating dinner. The kids were sitting by their father's feet while I sat beside him, a small but clear gap separating me from them. I felt like an intruder. *I did everything for them.* They were just children, I couldn't hold it against them. They would understand when they grow older. The voice nagged at the back of my head and I went to the medicine drawer to grab a paracetamol. My head was bursting in pain. I rummaged around clumsily inside tossing aside a thermometer, a bunch of Paul's medication, a ball of thread that we used to use to fly kites when we first got married. I found the paracetamol and took one and I turned around to see all three of them staring at me.

"Oh, I'm fine," I smiled, trying to play it off and they went back to watching TV.

Later, Paul asked me if I was okay and all I could do was think about those kites. What happened to them? Where were they now?

The next morning, everything went as per our new routine where Paul seemed to shoulder a lot of the work of getting the kids ready and dropping them off while going to work. I just sat in bed the whole morning, unsure what to do. I was still in my casual sleeping clothes, I had not even the will to brush my teeth. I made a cup of coffee for myself and stared at the TV as something played. I, then realized what I had to do. Those kites, I must find the kites. *Irene has those kites.* Yes, I gave it to her, didn't I? She must have wanted to show her kids how to fly a kite.

Despite my outer appearance, I took the scooter and went over to Irene's house which was about 10 minutes away. Every place in Pondicherry was 10 minutes away. I rang the bell and presented myself in all my morning breath, wrinkled old clothes and messy hair to... Jonathan, who answered the door. I suddenly became very self-conscious. I was not expecting him to be here.

"Oh, hey there stranger," Jonathan said with a wry smile, amused at my appearance.

I chuckled nervously. "Ummm, is Irene at home?"

"No, she just popped out. She'll be back soon."

"Okay. I just needed something from her."

"Come on in then, I'm sure she won't be long."

Yet again, God had given me the crossroads. The context was all in my mind, I knew what he wanted me to do but I did not know if I had the strength to do it. I was torn apart as always. I prayed for that moment of clarity that I got when I was at the hospital but for some reason it eluded me. *Just go in.* I went in.

I was not proud of what happened later but I knew it could never happen again. I told him that no one could know about it and said that I would ensure that we would never be alone together again.

I sat at home, waiting for my husband to return. The kids were playing inside while I contemplated what I should do. *I didn't mean it.* Yes, it meant nothing. But I still did it and now I had to own up to it.

There is no routine.

He returned home by 6 as he did every day now and was greeted by the kids. I sat and watched trying to control my emotions but I couldn't so I stormed into the bedroom and tried to breathe for a few minutes. Soon enough, Paul came in showing concern.

"Stop itt," I screamed at him. He backed off. "Stop being like this," I began to sob.

He didn't say anything.

"I understand," he said solemnly.

I built up the courage now and he was ready to listen. I apologized to him and then explained what happened. I told him it was impulsive and a one-time thing throwing all the excuses I had saying that no excuse could justify what I did too and he sat there and listened to everything. I was ready for anything. Perhaps he would even relapse and I would have to bring him back. I waited for his reply.

"Is it me?" he asked gently.

I started to cry and he put his arm around my shoulder but I pushed him away.

"Why aren't you mad? Say something, scream SOMETHING!" I cried out.

He sat there calmly and said, "I forgive you, dear."

"But why?" I sobbed.

"You stayed with me all these years and forgave me countless times, did you not? I am only returning the favor. How could I be mad at you? You have done nothing wrong your entire life. I believe you won't do anything wrong after this."

I took a moment to digest what was happening. This was so foreign to me. He was correct. I had been on the other side for so long that I had no idea what it was to be on this side. He tried to come over and hold me again but I pushed him away.

The audacity. I did not know what to do. I could not stay with this man, could I? He thinks he is better than I am. No. No. No. I could not do this anymore.

"I'm leaving," I told him defiantly.

"Darling, please—"

"NO! I AM LEAVING YOU! DON'T TOUCH ME!"

I stormed out of the room, went over to the kids' room, took Jacob in my arms, and grabbed Christian with my other hand but Christian resisted.

"We're leaving, Christian. NOW COME!" I screamed at him as Jacob began to cry and Christian shirked away in fear. Paul appeared in the doorway to block me and suddenly it was all too much. No no no no no no no. I tried to grab Christian again but he also began crying and Paul tried to say something to me but I heard nothing. AHHHHHH!

I did not know what was happening. I could not tell you now either, exactly what transpired. All I know for a fact is I did something to hurt my baby boy and I could not process it.

#4

I sat now in a bus station with a packed bag, trying to forget but also trying to remember. *What did I do?* I honestly could not remember anymore. Was my child okay? *I don't know.* I sat there without the will to move as my bus started. I had to get on. It rolled on away without me. I prayed but there was no meaning to words anymore. *The children. What were their names?* I broke down there, sobbing and sobbing but no one was around.

V

THE RED JOURNAL

The planet Earth was on the way back home so Steve and Brian decided to get tickets to visit all the attractions that remained. They got themselves enrolled in a tour while seeing the ashes of what used to be hailed as a thriving species. A race destroyed not by any force external but by their own flaws, which they claimed to be what made them better than us. The tour guide showed them the destroyed remains of various "Wonders of the World" so to speak as well as a few important members of their society.

A standout display was that of a Red Journal that belonged to a woman who lived in this civilization long ago, around what they referred to as the 21st century. The tour guide narrated the events that were mentioned in great detail to the attendees which included Steve and Brian who were fascinated.

After an enjoyable detour, they made their way back on course to their home planet but decided to make one final stop at "The Spacebar" where races and species from all planets were welcome to take a load off. Steve and Brian were so deeply touched by the story they heard from the Red Journal, it had to be taken off their minds. Though they said nothing to each other the whole journey, they were both in the same mind in wanting to get this off their minds to other members of the interplanetary society.

They ordered a drink and sat in silence for almost an hour. Then they looked at each other and nodded.

"Hello everyone, we have a story to tell you," Steve announced to anyone who would listen.

As was expected in a place like this, many attendees were more than happy to listen. The bar was designed in a way where people could gather around easily to listen to tales from each other with a central table surrounded by stools that were against a bar.

"Have you all heard of the planet Earth?" Brian asked.

There were a few murmurs here and there as well as a few nods and shakes of the head.

"Very well.

"This is the story we heard of the human being named "Grace" of "India", a "country" on the planet Earth back when civilization existed there in what they called the 21st century. She maintained a journal much like our travel logs of what she did in her short lifespan. We will now unload what has burdened us from hearing her story upon every willing listener." Brian announced.

Steve took over and began narrating her tale.

"This was the tale of a "girl", a "gender" that one was born with on this planet. I hope you are all familiar with the basic facts and practices that the Earthborn followed."

There were some nods and more murmurs.

"The tale begins when she began her journal entries at the Earth age of 9. She is very immature at this age and begins to talk about various silly little events such as meeting "boys" and "colouring". Her life seems to be encompassed around the love she receives from her father. She also seems to refer to a missing parental figure called the "mother". It is odd as she learns from other children her age that she is meant to have two parents. She cries to her "father" who only comforts her but never seems to be enough despite his best efforts.

Brian then took over, "The specifics evade our memory but she writes more about insignificant things and we call these insignificant because it is even acknowledged by her later on in the journal how silly her writing here is. She grows older and reaches a stage referred to by humans as "puberty". She is very confused. She writes in pain and shame. Her father cannot help her through no fault of his. She cries and shouts at him, later showing regret but only in the journal, never to him. She doesn't understand what is happening to her body or her emotions. She begins to make more and more bad decisions regarding the opposite gender "boys". This makes her more and more miserable but she continues anyway. This seems to be a phenomenon called "peer pressure". She watches her peers do and receive things and feels compelled to follow the same path."

Scattered laughter across the bar.

"Yes, quite silly, isn't it?" Steve said solemnly. "But no. Her pain and suffering at such petty, innate things is truly beyond our comprehension. Her entire life is turned around. Her search for a maternal figure never disappears but only grows more and more but she learns to hide it from her father who assumes she is truly satisfied with him. It is a painful narration to listen to her make bad decisions and find herself in situations where she lies and lies to the one, true person who cares about her. She grows older, finishing this system of education called school and joining yet another system of education called college. During this small transition, she seems to receive an enormous amount of enlightenment leading her to fix her relationship with her father."

"You seem to glaze over a lot of important points," a member of our audience pointed out.

"What specifics do you desire?" Steve asked. "We try to narrate as much as we remember."

"For starters, what is this invisible struggle that the girl had to go through that she could not speak with her father about."

"I believe there is a certain phenomenon which affects only women. It involves bleeding and pain that only they can bear from what we know."

"And what about this relationship with boys that she speaks of?"

"Well, it seems common with girls and boys of the ages 14-18 to engage in a relationship where they share sexual intercourse which was deemed premature by their society but their own pressures seem to force it and always seemed to end badly as was explained over and over in the journal."

"Might we proceed now?" asked Brian politely.

"Very well."

"As I was saying," Brian continued. "Upon entering this system of education called college the girl began to experiment with her life, find her place in society much like us. But she never seemed to find any contentment. On the outside, it appeared she only created problems for herself by entering into relationships with hurtful people but her thoughts show more complexity to her character. She is trying to fill this gaping hole in her life subconsciously and it is seen in the subtext of her words. Alcohol it seems was as popular there as it is amongst us as well as other substances that help humans feel high."

Some chuckles among the beings.

"She began to numb herself to everyone and everything and her father became nothing but a spectator in her downward spiral. Moreover, this was a very self-aware downward spiral. She writes about her malicious intent towards herself. The tragic downfall seems obvious in hindsight as we have seen humans as a self-destructive race and this Journal only enhances this notion. She speaks of ambition in bits and pieces, never sure of what she wants to do with her life but always written with conviction despite the constant change."

Brian paused as he exchanged glances with Steve.

"Well... go on." A stranger seated near them said.

"Perhaps I will narrate this next part," Steve took over. "She writes in great detail about a painful event in her life. At this point in time she has reached "adulthood" in Earth terms and is an independent living by herself in the same city as her father but scarcely speaks to him. She spends most of her time at work, writing about making a difference and justifying her long hours to herself. Her entries became dry for long periods and this was such a period. She then began describing an event involving fear, pain, and anxiety that she tried her best to enunciate with words. An event that brings clarity and enlightenment. An interaction with a co-worker in which she was subject to a plethora of mental and emotional stress that ended with her exploitation. She narrates her feeling of physical powerlessness through everyday life where she must always fear for her life as compared to her male compatriots. Her co-workers tried to exploit this weakness in her but she seemed to avoid any serious damage. She decides to drop everything, leave her job, her house, and move to a different place."

"Are there no real specifics to help us understand better?" someone asked.

Brian nodded and said, "To understand the specifics, you must be able to empathize with these beings."

Some muttering and chuckling.

"It appears they are not mature enough to understand so I believe we shall wrap up our story then," Steve told Brian.

The crowd began to disperse, leaving Steve and Brian to themselves. The stranger from earlier who asked for specifics approached them.

"Tell me, what more do you know about this?"

Brian nodded and said, "The historians who researched Earth believed that the unique dynamic between man and woman was meant to be one of perfection, a yin and yang but the corruptness of their civilization meant this was not to be. Instead, men and women were in constant battle with each other rather than embracing each other. This led women to live in constant fear as they were biologically much different from men which led them to be commonly exploited by men. The Red Journal speaks more on the institute of marriage which she later enters with small doubts in her mind. A man is intertwined with her for life and they are meant to procreate and propagate the human race. Again, the responsibility is meant to be shared, a bond between two people but this is not always the case. The Journal ends here but there are many theories based upon general human analysis on what her life may have been after that."

"I see. Truly, you have stirred my curiosity. I must pay a visit myself." The stranger left.

Brian and Steve sat there a little longer wondering what to do.

"We can never really understand, can we?" Steve asked.

Brian shook his head and took a sip of his drink.

VI

THE JOURNEY

An old lady by the name of Priya lived in an apartment building deep in the streets of Tambaram in Chennai. The distance from her apartment building to the main road was approximately 1.6 kilometres. She lived with her daughter, Mary, and her 7-year old grandson, Jeffrey. Mary and Jeffrey left every morning together at 7:30 AM with Jeffrey returning at 4 PM while Mary only came back by 8 PM.

Priya spent the entire day walking despite her daughter's initial protestations. Every day at 8 AM, she carried her walker and slowly made her way to the road. It was slow going for her as every day was. She stayed on the side while the world went on. The occasional school bus, the car on the way to the office, a bike, a scooter, and two men wearing laptop bags on a bike nodded as they passed her.

She greeted some of her neighbours who had grown used to seeing her walk this way. Some looked at her in pity, others ignored her while all she did was observe. All she could do was observe. The child waiting for his bus by himself, carrying his heavy lunch bag. The group of children with their parents, chatting amongst themselves. The golden retriever being walked by his middle-aged owner as he tried to control him from the chaos around. Priya trudged along ever so slowly. No rush. Not like the college student speeding across on his bike or the teenager running after the bus he just missed. One step at a time. She kept going.

Time kept flying past her as she made her way to the main road. She stopped several times to absorb her surroundings, bathing in the sunlight, embracing it. She had a pleasant conversation with Rachel, a homemaker she often spoke to on her route.

"Hi Aunty. How are we doing today?"

Priya just smiled and nodded.

"I have some of that ginger tea that you like. Care to join me?"

Priya perked up at the mention of this and nodded excitedly. She made her way into the compound of her house and sat on their balcony.

They both sipped their tea in silence. The world outside was quieter now.

"How's the tea, Aunty?" Rachel asked.

Priya was in a different time. She did not acknowledge her question, her eyes closed. She was thinking of all the different phases of her life during which she had ginger tea. At one point in her life, it represented her childhood and her dependence on her mother but that changed. She remembered when she began making it for herself and her mother. Soon enough, she was making it for her daughter. It always tasted the same. But it was different now. Or was it different before? She could not remember.

She finished her tea, said goodbye, and went on back to her slow walk to the main road. It was almost noon. The road was deserted except for the occasional bike. The sun did not bother her.

No one else bothered her. A couple of hours into the afternoon she had made her way to the main road.

The road began to grow around her. The sound of traffic and the people. She saw a couple fighting, two friends happy together, two cars coming head to head unable to decide who would make way for whom. The tea kadai marked the point of return. The smokers there took no note of her as they continued blowing smoke in her general direction while she tried to rest and catch her breath.

Now, the journey back awaited her. The chaos, she knew, would only grow. Her experience had told her as much. Nothing much changed from day to day. Human interaction grew dull and predictable yet she was a victim of it herself. She never thought of herself as someone who had attained peak enlightenment but her ability to decipher conversations between mother and son or friends or husband and wife merely from action was innately impressive to her.

Her journey back was a tad bit quicker as she made it back to her apartment in time for the sunset. She did not go back home yet. Jeffrey would be alone there but it was not her time to join him just yet.

She stood outside, watching the sunset. A boy was walking his Golden Retriever opposite her, the clouds were oddly shaped like her late husband, and the white house that stood in the middle of empty land was odd today. The two men on the bike with their laptop bags returned and nodded again at her as they went back to their respective families. It was not yet her time.

She walked down the road a little to an abandoned park and stood outside. She stared at the empty swing set, weeds growing everywhere, overgrown grass covering the dusty, broken seesaws. The monkey bars sat there empty, waiting for someone. She could not move. The park called out to her. She was not meant to go back home. She took a moment to make peace with this and opened the locked gate.

VII

LIFE LOUNGE

I woke up in a bar, a familiar bar. I took a moment to take in my surroundings while I wiped the drool and peanuts sticking to my cheek. It certainly looked like my usual place. The small, narrow corridor from the door led to a square opening with only two tables for four and a bar that was really more of a counter.

"Hello, there. Your usual?" Steve asked me from behind the bar.

Steve? How did I know his name?

He wasn't the usual guy but I still knew him.

"Is this—"

"The Evie special then."

How did he know?

"Yeah..."

I cautiously made my way to the bar, stumbling a little. He passed me my drink. The drink was named after me because of my expertise and regularity. Yet, this was not the place where I first created this. At first glance, it certainly did appear that way but no. I stared down at the violently pink drink in front of me. This was not the real Evie special. It couldn't be.

"Why am I here?" I asked the bartender.

"I'll let you figure that out."

Very helpful.

"You'll need this drink."

"Why?"

"To see everything."

That seemed unlikely given the amount of alcohol content in this could mostly make me see black. Nevertheless, I wasn't one to argue with the person telling me to drink so I drank the whole thing in one swell swig.

As expected, it went straight to my head and I shook it off. All right, then.

"You can go now."

I ignored him and made my way to the front door. I opened it to reveal the lush green landscape and clear blue skies straight out of some New Zealand nature documentary. Except for one crucial difference, there was something very primitive about these things, and standing in the middle of all this was a Dreadnoughtus and a Triceratops.

I closed the door and looked back at Steve who had vanished. Yeah, he definitely spiked my drink. That makes sense.

Why was I here?

I opened the door again, revealing a large lobby, a hotel lobby with some uniformed people and very few who weren't, the walls were a crimson red but the floors were lined with white tiles. The appearance was jarring.

My head grew lighter and almost felt like I was in a dream; my legs moved and my arms swung up and down but I did not feel in control. One of the uniformed men walked up to me and I could feel myself again.

"Baggage, ma'am?" he asked me.

I gave him a blank look but he stood there as if still expecting something.

"Do I look like I'm carrying anything?"

"Not the physical kind, ma'am."

"What other kind is there?" I asked realizing the answer to my question.

"Yes, ma'am. I'll take that, thank you." He said and walked away.

I felt so much better now. I had no hangover, my body felt a hundred percent, my mind was sharp and I had so much energy. Too much. I had no idea what to do with all of it.

I ran. I ran along the humongous, never-ending lobby unaware of anything around me until I reached the reception. At least, that's what it looked like.

"Welcome to the Life Lounge, what can I do to help you?" said the woman who spawned behind the counter.

Life lounge?

"Where time stands still so you can catch your breath. There is no concept of time here and you may return to where you left off in Earth anytime you wish and pick up right where you left off with a fresh perspective."

"What do I do now?"

"We have a number of red doors behind which you can find whatever you have been craving. Or you could just sit inside here for as long as you want."

This was perfect.

"Is that all then?"

"Yes, thank you." She vanished as mysteriously as she had appeared.

I made my around the lounge investigating different uniformed people who seemed to ignore me. I looked for other people who I had seen when entering but was unable to find anyone.

I found a buffet table with every type of food I could imagine, literally. Every time I thought of something, it appeared. *Tiramisu.* Voila. *Rib-eye Steak medium rare.* Voila. *Kinder Joy with the nostalgia.* Voila with the nostalgia.

Finally, I went up to the linc of rcd doors on the side, which were all unlabelled. I opened a random one, revealing the Bar. This time, the usuals were all there, except for me.

Why would this door lead me back to my self-pity hub of all places?

I reluctantly entered and felt a wave of something wash over me. It felt overwhelming but also comforting, it felt like the end of the world but something new awaited me. I was drawn to it. The discomfort, the pain, the *feeling* of it.

No one had noticed me as I slowly let go of the door and said goodbye to the Life Lounge.

VIII

THE END OF THE LINE

"I see you..."
"ICU, yes."
"Is it over?"
"Not yet, no."
"Why are you still here?"
"I... I just am."
"That's... That's okay."
Silence.
The blackness outside the window started to creep slowly through the walls.
"What is that?"
"I think you know."
"I- I don't."
Silence.
"You shouldn't be here."
"I know. But I am."
"Why?"
No response.

"Why?"

"Why did you leave me?"

"What?"

"Why?"

"I didn't want you. I didn't want any of that."

Silence.

"Don't go."

The blackness crept inside more and more.

"Please."

"I'm not."

"I never wanted this for you."

"Yet here I am."

"I- I can't apologize."

"No, you can't. It wouldn't do anything."

"I'm sorry."

"Shut up."

Silence.

"You can't blame me."

"Why not? My whole life has been shaped by you despite you not even being there."

"It wasn't my fault."

"Oh yeah."

"My father left me."

"That's a lie. Even now you lie."

"Yes. Even now you stay. Why?"

Silence.

"I don't want to know you."

"I gave birth to you."

"That's not why I'm here."

"But it's a reason."

"I don't need a reason. I am here for myself. To see you to your grave. To make sure you get no closure.

To ensure you die sad, old, shriveled and alone. Alone and afraid.

"But I'm not alone."

Silence as the blackness slithered along the ceiling.

"It's not too long now."

"I don't need closure."

"What?"

"I understand what I did. To you, to everyone. I know I'm a shitty person."

"No, you don't. You don't know the beginning of it."

"Perhaps. I know I don't deserve peace."

"Yes."

"But you do."

"I have it."

"Then why are you here?"

"TO SEE YOU DIE!"

Silence.

"Don't lie, son."

"I am not your *son*."

"I understand."

"What more do you want from me?"

"I never wanted anything from you."

"WHY NOT?!"

"I don't care about you."

"Why..."

"That's how life is. It's not fair. It wasn't fair to me and I chose to do this to you and has it not made you a better person in some way?"

"No, no it has not."

"Well, someone will be break the cycle, if not you."

The blackness covered half the room, it crept up the bed.

"I hate you. I hope you know that."

"I know."

"There is nothing after this."

"I know."

"Nothing."

Silence.

"You want me to regret."

"No."

"I don't believe in regret."

"Surprise, surprise."

"You should go."

"I will."

"It's everywhere now. I think I'm dead."

"Almost."

He wait earnestly as the bed, him and his mother remain to be the last bits that are sucked into the blackness.

"I have nothing to offer you."

"I never expected anything from you."

"I guess I won't see you on the other side."

"I never came to visit you, mother."

"I know."

She lets herself go.

VERMILLION

CONTENTS

Author – Hemanth

PREFACE

Life imprints itself on those that live it. Not all. Just those that genuinely want to listen to what life has to say. Much like that one good listener, who genuinely listens to what you have to say and doesn't just wait for you to complete so that they can share their opinion. These aren't just ideas or creations, they are much more than that. They are simple living truths of our life. These truths don't pop out on you; rather they wait for you at the door, not ringing the bell nor knocking. When you are ready for them, you find that you don't even have to open the door for them, for they are already sipping a cup on your couch.

To the fortunately unfortunate who are already exposed to this anagnorisis, which includes you too, dear reader, I hope to untell, tell and retell the stories that have imprinted themselves too intrinsically in me, that I have to try and re-imprint it on you, else they would eat me alive.

There are two kinds of purgation in my opinion; one is witnessing the spectacular or the grandeur as an entity outside of us or the macro (here the purgation is the realization is that, an event so grand might not happen to us, so we seek comfort in bearing witness to it). The latter is the everso ordinary and the mundane existence of life which still pleases us when represented outside, but really occurs within. Thus it is the micro, or as A.K. Ramanujan puts it, the micro which also has the macro within.

To please, I yearn to do, but to instruct, I dare not. At least not yet. Instead I pine to reflect and to relate.

To

nitin

kaaki

'Twas a rainy day in mid-December. The rain had been merciless on the Chennaiites for it had been pouring for the past 45 hours continuously, Ram was sitting in the waiting room for 25 minutes, anxiously tapping his feet. The light bulb was flickering heavily. Ankita, the managing director's secretary, walked in, looked him dead in the eye and said, "Ram, the board of directors will see you now." He stood up before she even finished her sentence, nodded at her and started walking towards the door. Little did he know that inside was the news that was waiting to tear his life apart.

As soon as he went in he saw 3 people, the MD, the CFO and the CEO. Ram sat himself in one of the chairs and looked at them earnestly. "Do you know why you're here Ram?" asked the CEO with all the prejudice in the world.

"I think I have an idea, sir" with all the pride he could gather.

"Well then, do enlighten us" said the MD mockingly. To this Ram said, "Is this about my raise, sir?" All three of them looked at each other for a split second and burst into laughter. Ram was now infuriated but equally confused. After a few seconds the CEO calmed down from his laughter, looked at Ram and said, "NO Ram, not even close. You're here to discuss the upcoming Nigerian Project. Well actually, we're here to tell you that Karim will be its TL."

It felt like all hell just broke loose into Ram's world. Not because he hadn't expected it but because he had. He knew all along that if it ever came down to both of them would be Karim every single time. It's not that Ram is not hard working, he actually works harder than anyone else in his organization, but he doesn't seem to have that finesse. It seemed that all that Karim touched turned into gold. Karim and Ram were the best of friends. They not only went to the same school, college and office but also to the same grocery store.

"We know that you and Karim are best friends, that's why we've called you. As we all know Karim unfortunately lost his wife just 3 months ago. What happened to him shouldn't happen to anyone else." Ram was nonchalant to all of this. Noticing this, the CTO said, "Ram we need you to give him this news personally. We know very well that he wouldn't accept it and that's why we need you to take him somewhere for a small vacation or something and make him understand how important it is for the company. I mean for Karim."

Ram, who had been silent until then, started speaking with a meek tone, "Sirs, you all know that

I work harder than anybody else in this office and I think I deserve a raise or a promotion or something"

"Ram" said the CEO speaking in an animatedly deep voice, "It's true that you work harder than anyone but you know deep down that you would never be able to do what Karim does and that's why he got the post and not you."

Ram was looking at them earnestly as though he wasn't convinced. So, the MD started speaking in a derogatory tone, "Look here, you get this done, we'll consider speaking about a raise. If not, well I guess it'll be the same old same old. Oh and to answer your question about the promotion that would only happen if Karim goes missing, or falls terribly ill or worse, dies". To this all three of them started laughing concomitantly as if it was supposed to be a joke. The cat got Ram's tongue. It felt as if he was choked so hard. It felt as if he was hit by a truck. It felt as if he was hit by reality.

Ram came out of the room with great difficulty and almost stumbled doing so. He looked for Ankita to ask for a glass of water but she was nowhere to be found. He found his way outside the Admin block and headed straight to a tea shop. This was the first time he regretted being a non-smoker. After drinking the tea he had ordered, he contemplated a plan to take Karim on a trip. The two of them had planned long before that they would visit Kolli hills on rented Royal Enfields. Ram may not have been a better employee but he was a good friend. He knew that the post was actually a once in a lifetime opportunity and would change Karim's life for good. So, he convinced Karim and their plan was to reach Koll hills by Christmas eve.

It was Christmas morning, they had rented a room at a hotel. Ram was asleep, Karim wasn't. In fact he hadn't slept a wink in the past 3 days nor did he have the intention of getting any shut-eye at all. He was gripping a red ball of yarn, thinking about her. Manisha was her name and in the past 3 months, it was her name that was ringing in his head above all the clamour of the world. He met her for the first time in his postgraduate course. It wasn't love at first sight. In fact he felt indifferent to her for the first couple of months. When he got to know her, it felt as though she was everything he wished to be but couldn't. He didn't know what exactly he felt for her but it was special. Manisha, fortunately not only knew what he felt for her but also reciprocated every single ounce of that feeling. They weren't a match made in heaven. They fought more often than not. It was their fights that made them formidable as a couple. This beautiful flush of memories was interrupted by the pallid thought of her corpse on the mortuary table. It was the sight that he wouldn't be able to unsee for the rest of his life. He looked down at her lifeless body, he was trying to cry so hard but it seemed as though all his nerves and muscles simply refused to respond. He was trying to contemplate what this sight meant. It signified that she had left him forever. It signified that her side of the bed would thereafter be empty. It signified that her footprints wouldn't be next to his on the sands of Marina.

It signified that she was no more

Manisha was kidnapped in broad daylight by a couple of small-time criminals, trying their hand at something big. They had asked for a 6,00,000 rupee ransom. Before Karim could arrange for the money, Manisha died in a gas leak along with her kidnappers. The kidnappers had left the stove on and unknowingly lighted a smoke which caused the gas leak to catch fire and all 3 of them died. Karim hadn't stepped out of his house for the past 3 months until the day before yesterday. It seemed as if he could shut everyone out except for Ram. That's why he agreed to come on this trip. Karim was again disturbed from his train of thought by the sound of Ram waking up.

"Kari, we always go to the Aagaya Gangai waterfalls, let's try something new, no? Moreover the trek to the waterfalls is as dry as dust. This time we'll do something interesting, there's this place... it's called Valappur Agaya Gangai falls top view. We'll see the same waterfalls but from the top. At least now, we get a shift in perspective. Besides, it's a good spot to have the first alcoholic drink of my life" said Ram trying to convince Karim.

"Ram is trying alcohol. We are surely in the Kaliyug.

Can you not drink alcohol? Then maybe we'll go to the spot you suggest"

"Okay okay, we should get started now if we want to come back from the place before dusk". Both of them had been walking for 15 minutes, when they reached the place and Karim saw that Ram wasn't kidding. This place was amazing and the view was simply spectacular.

But Ram wasn't here just for the view. No.

He's here to change the course of his life. When Ram came out of the admin block that day something changed in him. Something broke. And after he had that tea he had, he lit up the first smoke of his life. That smoke was Ram yelling out to the rest of the world, "I've had enough of being the nice guy." The constant pain of underappreciation had gotten to him. He needed that chance more than Karim. Karim wasn't the one with orthodox parents who compares their son with others who earn more; Ram was. Karim wasn't the one whose girlfriend left him for a richer guy; Ram was. He was now ready to do anything to get that job and to get that money. By anything he was even ready to kill his best friend. So that's what he planned to do. The ignorant MDs offensive remark about Karim had clenched his mind like an anchor that grasped the seabed.

"I know you told me not to try my first drink here, but technically this isn't my first drink, and I've been drinking heavily for 4 months to forget all my sorrows" said Ram as he took a Swiss knife, a glass, a water packet, a pickle sachet and some liquor. Karim was lost for words when he saw this happen. He gathered himself and spoke angrily, "Why did you lie to me, Ram?"

"I've been interrupted my whole life, but not today. Listen to me carefully. You know that I am the nicest person one could find. You yourself told me so. Let me tell you something, Kari, being nice isn't fun.

Your parents call you naive, your girlfriend leaves you, you always eat last in the family, and people use you knowing that you won't say no if they ask for help. You never get a seat in the bus, and I can go on and on and on and on, Kari. You might say that all this is my choice, well that's true, a choice that I'll regret till my grave. You know what's the worst thing about it, Kari? They make fun of your pain. You can make fun of many things about a person but if they make fun of your pain, that's when things can get ugly. Uglier than anyone can imagine. So ugly that one wonders if this person is really capable of doing this. I'll show them... I'll show them that... I too am capable of things unimaginable. Do you know why we're here? The board of directors called me and asked me to give the news to you that you've been made TL. Do you know how deep it hurts me to say that, I worked so hard for that job that even the office boy knows that I should be next." ranted Ram. His excessive smoking had caused him to run out of breath.

"But, Ram, I don't want that Job, you can have it if you want," said Karim in an assuring tone. This seemed to have angered Ram.

"What did you say? Do you think I'm here to eat your leftovers, to clean up your shit, to be second? Guess what? You're right. But they won't even let me do that. I can't get that job unless you're dead, Kari. Karim... Please I beg of you with all my heart, please Kari, jump off this cliff and die. Please do it so that I won't have to kill you to get that job. Please do this for me". Karim was not shocked by this at all. It was as if he was waiting for this to happen. Karim looked Ram dead in the eye and spoke calmly, "Ram I've known you for about 23 years. You never miss my birthday. You always give me a gift every single year. It's only fair for you to give me the gift of death. But I'll not do it myself. You have to deliver the coup de Grace, you have to wrap the gift yourself. No backsies." Ram's brain was too slow to understand what just happened. After a full minute Ram burst into tears.

Karim spoke more quietly than ever, "shhh... there... there, it's ok. I'm ready to see Manisha.

"Thank you for being my friend, Ram". On hearing this Ram started crying even more. Slowly he moved towards him. Took a shovel which he had placed there earlier that day and hit Karim 45 times on the head repeatedly.

Karim had died at about the 23rd blow. The whole time he was looking at Ram, not with anger, not with regret, but with contentment, and closure.

Ram had stopped crying. He poured himself the drink and drank it like a beast that hadn't seen water for years.

Before taking a seat under the tree shade, he noticed a piece of paper sticking out of Karim's pant pocket. Ram fetched it and sat down next to Karim. When he unfolded the paper and read it, his heart sank. It was a letter to Ram by Karim. The letter read:

Dearest Ram,

I know that we're here because I am going to be the next TL. I know that you're going to kill me. I also know that you have been drinking alcohol for the past 4 months. I saw you leave early in the morning with a shovel. That is how I found out how desperate you were for, well, everything. I don't blame you for killing me, Ram.

I blame you for killing Manisha. What? You don't know what I'm talking about? Let's rewind the clocks, shall we?

It was the 5th of October. At 10:35 in the morning, Manisha landed in Chennai. I was supposed to go pick her up. I couldn't. I tried to, but the goddamn traffic delayed me. At 11:34, 1 called you 45 times. You weren't at the office, you didn't pick up my calls. You were drinking at a bar. So, she started for home on her own. I left you 45 missed calls and in the next 45 minutes, precisely at 12:19 in the noon Manisha was kidnapped. You killed her, Ram. You killed my Manisha. You took away the lone hope of my life, Ram. She was my light Ram and you made me blind.

Now I'm gonna make sure that you search for an ounce of light in a chasm of darkness. So, I spent the next 3 months in isolation to re-engineer the strychnine toxin to kill a person when ingested within 45 minutes. It's very painful and that's why I didn't want to see it happen. So I mixed it in your alcohol. I asked you not to drink, didn't I? But I know you will drink it, and you will die soon. Very soon. I know you killed me for other reasons. Well, Ram, I'm pleased to say, what I did to you was purely personal. My love for you has reduced greatly but a few ounces are still left. Therefore I departed before you.

Until I see you down there,

With dwindling amounts of love

Karim

As he finished reading the blood stained letter which was now stained with Ram's tears, he looked at Karim, and then he looked at his watch. He then sat there without taking his eyes off of what was left of Karim's head. The whole time he had a perpetual smile on his face. Precisely 45 minutes after he had taken the drink, he fell beside Karim breathing his last.

finis.

II

MEMOIRS OF A LOVER

I was born in the Himalayas in the spring of 1910. The sights that welcomed me into this god forsaken planet were too misleading. As misleading as a chocolate given to a child before taking it to the dentist. The lush green friends of mine, the deadly white far off yet so close at the same time, and all my lovely tenants were on time with their rents. I had nothing to complain about. Life was good.

Do you ever have this feeling that everything is good? Probably too good that sometimes you start anticipating something bad might happen. I had been having this anxious feeling for a long time. And finally after 33 years on a fatefully grateful day after rains, the human cut me down. Sometimes I'm not really sure whom to denounce or whom to vent my anger on. My creator or my destroyer. Thanks to my destroyer I at least got to meet a lot of people. But only Prapanjan stood out. He stood up and sat down forever in my heart, anchoring himself with millions of strands entwined, made up of the same matter that makes the ether that makes you. Makes me. Makes us.

Prapanjan.

After killing me the human cut me up into pieces and sent me to different places. The first piece I remember is the cradle that Prapanjan's father bought. He was so happy when he found me and was ready to take me home. The first day I saw Prapanjan, it was as though the universe actually came to see me. His eyes lit up the room. A single drop of light in an abyss of darkness still illuminates. Still glimmers. Still brings hope.

Prapanjan was my first light, my daybreak. His constant whines never seemed odd to me although it disturbed his mom much. I don't know how, (probably someone up above or down below knows) but even after growing out of the cradle I kept meeting Prapanjan in various different ways. My second piece that I remember was a wooden parrot toy. In a Tamil-film like coincidence, it was Prapanjan's toy again. But this time around something was off. Something was wrong with my Prapanjan. He seemed discontent. He was joyful, he was happy, he was cheerful but something was missing. I was dying to know but there wasn't a way I could find out. Oh if only I could speak.

Days passed like grains of sand through the fingertips. No news of Prapanjan. I had almost given up. I started meeting other mediocre people who seldom excited me.

The next piece was different. Somebody held me, it was familiar. They sharpened my edges for some reason. Then I knew. It was him. My heart skipped a beat. Hm, do I have a heart? He was now about 5ft tall and wrote something with me. I knew then that he wasn't too smart but that didn't matter. His eyes were the same. They looked like they could provide electricity for China for 200 years and still have that light. But something was not right even now.

But I didn't know.

Years went by like the days of the summer holidays that children have.

It was dark for a long time. Then I saw some light. There were several pieces of me together. It was him again. I felt as though all my branches oozed with love. Hm am I capable of love?

He took one of my small parts and struck me against something else. I suddenly caught the red flower. He took me and the red flower close to his mouth where he had a small white stick which took the red flower and gave off some smoke. I couldn't breathe. But that was okay, because he was there. As long as he was there I felt like a child in the grasp of her mom. It could never hurt me. He could never hurt me.

It would be best by far if all beings were born infallible by nature, but things don't often go that way. He too had a flaw. Neeli. That unholy communion took place in front of me. That wretched priest recited hymns to sanctify their marriage in the flames and the embers that came from my destruction. Even then I felt that Prapanjan was not complete. Something was missing. I wish I could know.

This time, even Time was cruel to me. It took its time. Sometimes I really think that if I ever had another lifetime I would've been a writer. 4 decades had passed. Decades for him, eons for me. But it was all worth it.

One unfortunately fortunate day, I felt someone stacking many pieces of me together with a rope and finally some 4 people kept something heavy on me. The moment the shroud touched me. I knew it was him. But something was different this time. He was more complete than before, more dynamic, although his physical vehicle was static. I just wanted to ask him what it was that he was searching for, for so long and whether he found it or not. Sure enough, he told me.

They all took him on their shoulders and started walking. That witch, Neeli started acting as though she was crying and most of them fell for it too. They proceeded to carry him to some place and they set him down. Then they started sticking more pieces of me on him. Another man, I think it was his son, started walking around his father. I almost laughed. But after that he took his red flower and kept it on me. That's when it hit me. Prapanjan was leaving this unholy planet. Good for him. Suddenly something changed. Something clicked. I felt Prapanjan opening his eyes. He looked at me and smiled. The red flower burned through me, a piece of me, burnt but full of love fell on his lips. That was what he was searching for.

He was searching for me.

Slowly one by one they all started to leave. I too one by one was turning into embers and more importantly he was subsumed in me. Finally we came to my last piece. The last ember. It was bright but not brighter than his eyes. Which shone then and shines now. After a few hours even my mother Earth couldn't separate us. His son then took us to the beach and mixed us in the huge waters. That was it. Now we were in each and every last drop of that water. I couldn't hold back my tears and neither could he? So we cried and cried until the sweet water turned salty.

finis.

III

THE BROWN EARTH AND THE POURING BLOOD

Twas a day after a night of rain. The skies seemed to be even more clear than they normally appear. The blue sky was hardly blue, for it was almost white. This was even more strange because the previous day it had been outright black. Not orange, not red, not even that gloomy grey that seems to put almost everyone in a slumber. It was just black. Plain black. Blacker than your hair gets, after that 15 minute dye on the commercials. The black mom had finally given birth after struggling in labor for 12 hours straight. She was mostly relieved but was also happy. Her happiness was infectious as it made all the people of Chennai wet. Some were willing, most weren't. But the black mom didn't care.

Jude woke up to this wonderfully white morning in an unusually blue mood. Why? He just couldn't figure it out. Like most times. His father, however, had an answer. He strongly suggested that the reason was the theatre company that Jude has newly joined. Deep down, Jude knew that his dad might be right, but he quickly squashed that thought. As quickly as you would squash an innocent ant on its way home. Not because he was a predator, but because that thought was true. He didn't feel home at the theatre company. He had this quiet uneasiness in the deeper gorges of his mind. It was very feeble, but was constant. Like the slight rain that very slowly but surely pounds the Earth, but never wears out. This slow, constant pounding of the uneasiness had perhaps foreshadowed the painful things the future had in store for him.

"It's not like you think pa. I am having a blast there", lied Jude effortlessly.

Well, to be fair, it wasn't a complete lie. Like every other lie in the world, there was some truth in it. The blast was there. It just wasn't him, that was having it. His theater company is an apt example of all intent and no form. It was a 25 year old company. Anything that ages too much has one small issue. Sometimes, people get stuck in the past. The company had this same flaw and some more. Insecure, powerful people. The oppressors oppressing the oppressed is bad. But the traumatized ill-meaning oppressed, wielding newfound power is nothing short of Pandemonium.

Like he always does, Jude let a lot of air explore him, and set the thought aside.

He made up his mind and bed and got ready for the day. After a pretty meaningless day, uncommon to him, he made it to the company. Same blast, same radius, same casualties. It gives a lot of pleasure to those that suffer, to suffer with company. Jude found a companion of misery that day. To be accurate he had already met him, but this setting was more ... dramatic.

The first time Jude met him was in fact, in a completely different setting. It was shortly before a wave of happiness hit Jude, that he met Nitin for the first time. Like all games created by the limited human mind, one always triumphs but at the cost of another's tears. Jude's triumph, however, came at the expense of Nitin's indifference. Jude was taken aback. Never had Jude seen such nonchalance in a limited human face before, but there was still a genuine happiness that Nitin had for Jude's victory. In a conversation he had with Nitin, shortly before the results of the meaningless game was announced, Jude tried to make out what kind of a person Nitin was. As you associate every person you know with a colour, Nitin was brown. Both literally and metaphorically.

The colour brown is a very subtle colour, Jude always thought. His father mostly wore black belts and shoes, but for some reason, Jude preferred the rare days when his dad wore the brown belt. It was more chic for all the reasons in the world. Not blunt like black but persistent and smooth. The picture of the dry woods, the furniture in his room, a lonely carton box in an otherwise empty room. These things gave Jude the calm he needed.

Nitin studied philosophy and this was something so strange to Jude. As strange as the first time, a kid discovers that tomato is a fruit. How could you study philosophy? Do you just think during the class hours with an existential crisis for the short break? It amused Jude. So much so that he entered a conversation with Nitin about Gene Jacks Rousseau. Or at least that's how Jude pronounced it. Nitin was quick to correct him,

"It's Jean-Jacques Rousseau!" interrupted Nitin. As surprised as Jude was about what he had said, Nitin apologized to Jude, "Not to correct you, but that's how they taught us." For some weird reason, as weird as this encounter was, Jude thought that he had found a friend that night.

Jude was genuinely pleased to see Nitin at the company. It was like that feeling you have, when your parents make you go to this lame family get-together and you're having the worst time. Just when you think that you have run out of means to save your evening, you see that one cousin who actually gets you. Jude quickly ran over to him to say hi, but it wasn't until he got near Nitin that it struck Jude that he might not remember him. Pausing for a moment, he composed himself and tapped Nitin on the back, " Heyy Nitin, remember me?"

Nitin turned around and greeted him with a smile. Just as Jude was about to say something, Nitin started singing, "Hey Jude, don't make it bad. Take a sad song and make it better." By this time Jude had reddened incredibly, feeling embarrassed. Obviously he hadn't heard the song before. Sensing this Nitin quickly stopped and greeted Jude properly. Turned out Nitin too was finding this new place tough, though it wasn't as depressing to him as it was for Jude.

No sooner had Jude got home, than he heard, "Hey Jude" on a loop several times. He absolutely fell in love with the song. After that, whenever he thought life was unfair to him, he would hear that song. Every time he heard that song, it reminded him of Nitin.

It would take Jude 3 years, after Nitin's death, to listen to this song without his tears drenching his cheeks without his consent.

Jude wasn't the closest friend of Nitin, nor was he an occasional one. You ever meet these people, who you spend time with because you are put in situations with them. Be it the same class that you both took, catching a glance of each other while you pass each other by... Things like that. Jude and Nitin were that type of friends.

After spending a year in the theatre company, Jude quit. He lasted that long, solely because he was too dedicated to ditch it halfway through. After that, Jude wouldn't see him for another semester or so. Until one day, they found out they were going to share a Gender studies class with each other. Although, this time around Jude couldn't see Nitin as often as before. Like every other petty thing that happened in Jude's life, he didn't give it much thought. Moreover, he was too busy with life to make note of such things. Whenever Jude saw him in class, once in a fortnight or so, he made it a point to at least share a hello, although it was as meaningless as the dividers in our geometry boxes. Jude would casually ask him, "So, how's life?"

"Terrible", Nitin always used to reply with a big smile. So of course, Jude took it as sarcasm or just another 'divider' type answer.

Time was cruel to Jude. It ran from him like his school crush did, when he tried to approach her. The frequency that he saw Jude decreased constantly and it didn't seem to bother Jude at all. Why should it?

Until one morning on a random Whatsapp check, he saw Nitin's picture on the Chairperson's status. His heart sank. Sank so quickly, that Titanic took eons when compared to his heart. He knew that the Chairperson doesn't keep people's pictures on her status for their Birthdays. That left only one option out. With great difficulty, Jude opened the Chairperson's status. There was a picture of Nitin and down below the description read, "We regret to inform you that nitin..." Jude didn't have to read the rest. He put his phone down and closed his eyes. No sooner had he closed his eyes, than the memory of meeting him just two days ago was thrust upon Jude. Jude was walking towards the gate and Nitin was going towards the main block. He was flushed and his eyes were swollen so big that it looked so odd on his normal sized frame even from a significant distance. Jude stopped to talk to him, Nitin didn't. "How are you?" asked Jude. "Dead" said Nitin, "I was at the other block in class, but I overslept, now I'm running there". Jude smiled at his answer and bade him adieu.

He had to know what happened. He picked up his phone and called up the chairperson, "They're not sure yet, but they think that it was suicide", she said, choosing her words as carefully as a politician would in a press meet after a riot or a grave disaster.

He opened his eyes and crumbled up like the first bite of the puffs that you get in every other bakery. Never before had Jude cried so hard. He cried for an hour straight. His father was so confused and when Jude told him, he naturally thought that it was a very close friend of his and that's why he was crying so much. His dad stayed with him for a little while and tried to console him, but nope. No piece of information, no detail about him, not even the truth about the origin of the universe was going to console him.

He went to his class, sat alone and waited for one of his very few sensible classmates to come. He then spoke to him alone about Nitin. Truth has many versions. "Every damned dimwit that had a mouth, has something to say about him.

'Oh he always used to go away for a week and then suddenly come back', 'He has a twin, so he couldn't bare to be away from him', but nobody actually gives a shit", cried Jude to his mom.

To those who didn't know him, he was an interesting topic of conversation, some good-hearted souls genuinely felt sorry for him. But that's it. After a couple of weeks, nobody, save a few of his actual friends seemed to notice that he was gone. Perhaps it was because they didn't notice when he was there too.

For Jude it was different. He knew that Nitin wasn't very close to him, but he couldn't come to terms with the fact that nitin was no more. How much weight does these words have, 'being no more'. What does it mean? That nitin will no longer walk the roads that kiss the woods, that he can no longer laugh at a lame joke cracked by his dumb friend, that he cannot feel the delightful taste of water when it hits his tongue after being thirsty for hours, that the spring morning's wind will no longer caress his cheeks, but will for the others, that the summer morning's cuckoo will now sing its hymns to life, but no longer for Nitin. For now he is with them. Where do they all go? Does the promised Paradise really await us? Or do the nine rings of hell wait impatiently for his sentence? Or is he in the ether that fills the mountains that run tirelessly beside the river of sin and good deeds, in the ether that exists between the lips of a mother about to kiss her newborn's forehead that sleeps peacefully in the cradle at the hospital, in the ether that fills you?

Or is he with Jude?

The moment his earthly body was cut by the circular demons of the vehicle that run on parallel lines, his blood fell on the brown earth, but this brown earth was not of Nature, and so it didn't hold on to the blood drop. As the drop dripped and parted ways with the brown Earth, at that exact moment all of Jude's earthly ties with nitin were cut. At that exact moment, there was a nitin shaped hole, that neither memories and elegies, nor ether itself can fill. At that exact moment, this hole was also a part of Jude.

Deep down in the recesses of this hole, Jude always hears the faint echoes of nitin's voice softly singing

"Hey Jude, don't make it bad. Take a sad song and make it better."

"Hey Jude"

Finis

IV

A RANDOM UNNECESSARY THING

"Open your eyes." said a voice to Karnan. It hurt. To open his eyes, to even send a command from his brains, through his nerves, to his eyelids for them to try and push themselves up. With utmost difficulty, with one half of an eyelid open, Karnan tried to make up for the other half by lifting his head half-up. It was blurred. A random unnecessary memory of how he used to press his eyes long enough, so that his eyes would become blurry and he would be able to see the other dimensions, thumped its way into Karnan's mind. It wouldn't be for another five minutes, that Karnan, very slowly, managed to make out who or what was in front of him. For that full five minutes, the someone or something in front of him stood as an embodiment of Saburi (patience).

It was a man. Was it a man? He looked... odd. Not man-like. Or even human-like for that matter. But you would have to look at him for a full minute to notice his oddity. Otherwise he was what filmmakers would call 'atmosphere'. The fact that, in a film, we don't notice anyone else except for the main characters, save the occasion, that the filmmaker wants us to notice them, always bothered Man. How could it be? Man could understand the fact that it is the story of the protagonist that she was there to witness and it was the story of the protagonist that the filmmaker wanted to tell. Apart from that, what about the dude bringing tea to the hero? What's his story? Why is he selling tea? A random unnecessary detail that would result in nothing but further complication or even a waste of precious time.

Man noticed that Karnan had noticed Man, who had zoned out. Pulling herself back to her senses, Man looked at Karnan with the most sincere gaze. It was accompanied by something you could qualify as a smile. It was the gaze of the mother who had just brought a thing alive into this world and is now looking at it with utmost attention. Jumping out of the rapt that Man had put himself into, he spoke. Karnan could see that Man was moving her mouth but it was as if the audio wire wasn't plugged into one of those beautiful many coloured holes on the television. After some struggle, he was able to make out what Man was saying. He seemed to be saying,

"Karnan, dear. Can you hear me? Does it hurt?"

The choice of vocabulary that Man had approved, inadvertently triggered a memory for Karnan. A forgettable one. One about his mother. The peculiarity was that it was as though his mother had chosen to speak in Man's voice. The words, the inflections, the tone. Everything was the same. Even the love.

Karnan was now slowly trying to shake off his fatigue. After looking at himself and realizing that he was fastened to the chair that he was made to sit on, with some sense, he asked Man,

"Who are you? Where am I? Why am I tied to this chair?"

To this Man, smiled. It was more than a smile, but hardly a laugh. That smile/laugh reminded Karnan of his History teacher. He used to do that exact same thing after cracking what qualified to him as a joke and the non-Emersons in the class would laugh to please. But not Boy. Boy never laughed. Not for the history teacher, not for anyone.

"You're thinking about that history teacher, aren't you?"asked Man, derailing Karnan's train of thought. This shook Karnan, more than he had ever been shook in his life.

How could Man possibly know the History teacher. Man was too old to be Karnan's classmate. Too young to be the History teacher's spouse. That brought him back to ...

"NO! It couldn't be!" Karnan shuddered within himself. A shudder that was felt in each Mitochondria of each of his cells. Mitochondria was the powerhouse of the cell. His Biology miss had taught him. He hoped that this fact would somehow save him from the terrible memory that was gushing past his will into his conscious. From Jung's personal subconscious to Karna's Freud's Libido.

He had killed the powerhouse of his life. The fountain from which the energy in his body emanated, he had demolished. Vandalised. Sinned. Beyond redemption. An unchristian Sin beyond mercy. "You remember me now, don't you dear?" asked Man in a tone unchanged from her first sentence. Again Karnan was brought back from his deep train of thought. He was almost at Tirumalpur, when Man's voice summoned him back to Tambaram. Or Tambaram Sanitorium, rather.

"Yes, uh ... I think. Why... Why are you calling me 'dear'?

With his archetypal smile, Man didn't rush to answer. She revealed, " I have kidnapped you in broad daylight from your own house. I have sedated you for the past 72 hours. In that 72 hours I have done you the favour of gouging one eye and reducing the weight of your right leg and left arm from the weight of your body. Yet the random unnecessary thing that bothers you is me calling you 'dear'?"

Karnan was flabbergasted. He came to the undesirable realization that Man was right. He did have only two of his four limbs and he had no control of his right eye whatsoever.

"Hai. Haaai. *^%$@#! Who do you think you are? Do you know who I am? Do you even have the slightest idea of what you have done?" sweared Karnan.

"Do you, Karna?" started Man dramatically for the first time.

Karnan was dumbstruck. He couldn't understand what or why on earth this was happening to him. He was still trying to make sense of this incredibly senseless situation. The fact that he had lost an arm, a leg and an eye, but still was in no pain however, confused Karnan to a great extent. He looked at the places where his limbs used to be, it was neatly tied up in a white bandage. There was no sign of blood. It was professionally done. Karnan couldn't but admire the art in the work Man had done. When he was almost sucked into that stupid thought, he shrugged himself back to reality. He was now a little more calm, but still as tense as a person who lost two of his limbs ought to be.

"Why?" he cried to Man. Man was emotionless. It seemed as though she was waiting for this moment his whole life. But he put off that moment a little while.

" Do you know my name, Karna?" uttered Man, with a look that already knew the answer to the question.

"I know you." answered Karnan, presumptuously.

Man burst into laughter like innocent children do. Without a care in the world. Without the guilt of having amputated a man.

" I'm not going to lie, but that is one of the most hysterical things I have ever heard. And take it from a wom...uh a man who has spent quality time with hysterical people, that is a good one." finished Man with a follow-up laugh but now he appeared a little uncomfortable.

"Now coming to your question. The right one. Not who, but why? Now if you will, I have undergone a great deal of hardwork and pain for this. So, kindly pay attention." said Man, pulling out a paper that was torn unevenly from its home. It was yellow. It was brown. It had that blot that only time presents papers. He unfolded with a sanctimonious sincerity and began reading a poem.

The poem read

Four score years ago,
Mother planted a tree.
Little did she know
That it would be me.

The seeds did she sow;
She thought would make glee
Dying to see me grow,
She saw, but couldn't be.

Two score years ago,
Met a boy called Thee.
All me sorrows did go,
So did a part of me

One score years ago
Thee made me glee.
Dainty was it, head to toe
A plant beneath a tree

Little did I then know
We'd have to pay a fee
The tree did then go
Sadly, without me

The plant did hack him down
Dissolved him in the sea
Now, before you go,
Do you remember me?

He did indeed.

Man finished his reading of the poem. He was very excited. The excitement that you have, when you sketch your family for the first time and show it to your mother in great anticipation and she puts it up on the refrigerator. Karnan on the other hand was slowly losing his consciousness. The time seemed as though it was stitched to meet the turn of events. No sooner had Man completed his poem, than Karnan was falling into his sleep again.

The fall was steep. As steep as, when you're rocking a chair, and in one rock you go too far that you lose control of the rock. So now you have to catch hold of something in order to not fall. That steep. But as he was slipping into his sleep, he remembered the random, unnecessary, terrible thing that he had done to Man.

Karnan was almost completely engrossed by his sleep. Just then, Man burst into a song. His voice unexpectedly was the most beautiful alto Karnan had heard. But he had heard it before. Slept in it before. Done a terrible wrong to it before.

செஞ்சோற்று கடன் தீர்க்க
சேராத இடம் சேர்ந்து
வஞ்சத்தில் வீழ்ந்தாயடா, கர்ணா!
வஞ்சகன் கர்ணனடா!

வருவதை எதிர்கொள்ளடா, கர்ணா!
வருவதை எதிர்கொள்ளடா!

To repay the debt of sustenance
Thou has reached where one must not.
Thou has been deceived, Oh Karna!
The deceiver is Karnan!

Embrace your destiny, Oh Karna!
Embrace your destiny!

finis.

V

THE DEATH OF THE MOTH: A MODERN ANTIGONE

(Dear reader, this short work is a product of engaging with Sophocles's text for more than 6 weeks for the stage and the impact the essence of the text had on my crew. Therefore, this story substantiates what a text/character does to the actor that dons the role.)

Twas a hot September day. A little too hot for September, one would reckon. There he was looking straight ahead, a two thousand year soul trapped in a twenty one year old skin. Creon felt nothing, as he looked on at the professor who was talking endlessly about something not so very interesting.What happened next even Zeus couldn't explain at first.

A moth had entered the classroom through the window. It all happened so quickly. Quicker than clock's tick but slower than maggie. Creon had noticed the moth, but as he yelled, 'Switch off the fans!' the moth had flown into one. The modern Icarus had fulfilled its purpose, but Creon wasn't ready to let go. He quickly tried to pick it up but the moth was reluctant, more reluctant than Antigone herself. It was only then that it struck him. It was time. He hesitated no more. He picked it up, almost against its will. But as soon as he did, it stopped moving. It tried to hold on to Creon's fingers with all of the might of Zeus. He slowly moved out of the classroom and placed it on the floor. It struggled. Flapped its wings not in denial but in acceptance. Suddenly all was still. She struggled no more. Witnessing this broke something in Creon. Something that had become as hard as a rock for many millennia.

He picked up the moth that breathed no more and rushed outside the building. He digged, digged and digged, and finally buried her. He closed the pit. Without waiting for his consent, one tear, the embodiment of a two thousand year old guilt, fell exactly on top of the heap of sand.It was as though she had forgiven him. It was as though Antigone had forgiven him. He was ready now. Ready to let go.

finis.

VI

ITTEFAQ (COINCIDENCE)

Twas a gloomy day in September, in the year of our lord two thousand and fourteen. Whose lord? That Gautham didn't care about. When Gautham woke up at a guilty late time, he looked upon the sullen skies which seemed to reciprocate his mood. He tried to reach for something on his bed, when his mother's ball of yarn caught his hand. She had stitched his shirt overnight.

He liked these kinds of days. The sun which is forever more gracious on the people of Chennai, seemed to take a half hearted break. Neither here, nor there. On the contrary, the rain was scornful to the people. The rain was stingy yet teased the husbands who wanted to dry the washed laundry.

Gautham had just graduated the toughest, most demanding class of 5th grade and was stepping into a new world of middle school. He was what some would call 'privileged', others 'lucky', but most people called him '*samathhu*' or 'obedient'. It wasn't until 9 years later, until he went through Emerson's sermons,would he discover that he was what Emerson called 'a conformist'. No one had an issue with him. Not his parents, not his grandparents, not the distant relatives that don't genuinely give a hoot about other people's lives, but just eat people at dinner conversations. The childless couple for appetizers, the unhappy divorcee for the entree, and to finish up with the failed child borne out of ineffective parenting for desert. Not even those venomous beings had a problem with Gautham. Not his friends, not his teachers, not even his enemies. The entirety of his puny world seemed to function with him, like a newly greased old cycle, save for the exception of himself.

There were these random moments, too random in fact, either when he was on a bike ride with his dad, when he was looking at a sunset, but mostly when he was doing nothing. Unfortunately 5 star wasn't there to save him. He would have these epiphanies, or rather the antithetical version of it, for it brought nothing but took away everything that he had. He was lost for words, thoughts, even images. He would anxiously look at his hand to forcefully summon an unrelated thought, but no. His cognition was on a transient harthal. The only thing on his mind that can be described in words is, What is all of this and why on Earth am I here?

Apart from these uninduced trips into the other dimensions, everything else about Gautham was normal. Until that day came for him.

Before you live through that day, reader, it is important for you to know about an important person. Paapa. Paapa was 69 years young when she died. 61 years old in the year of our lord two thousand and fourteen. Paapa was Gautham's father's father-in-law's lawfully wedded wife. Paapa loved Gautham, the way a child loves not just the flower but also the plant. Because if the love was only for the flower it would pluck it for a few greedy sniffs. But Paapa nurtured Gautham,with specially bought potassium nitrate fertilizers. Is it because people only love the plant for the flower, that they run out of love, when the plants run out of flowers?

The Gautham plant loved Paapa no matter. With an innocence of a puppy that loves the boy on his street, with a relief that you get after being sick for a week, with a comfort that lovers have when they rest their heads on their only ray of hope, in the comfortable metros or judgemental electric trains at the end of a long day.

Never in all the *did you know?* that Gautham had to study, (for they especially asked questions from there) did he learn that one single event could change almost everything in your life, even your diapers. On that half-hearted September day, there were no crows that fought with the squirrels, no dogs that were promiscuous, nor were there eternally hungry cows that took whatever you gave them, superseded in that ability only by soil. Gautham was empty.

There was only one thought, the nervous anticipation of something bad that was going to happen. To be brutally honest, deep inside, Gautham wanted something to happen. Something interesting. Something dramatic. But not to him. Like a bomb that goes off at a safe distance from you. You feel sad, but you can't help your basic instincts feel that fascination for catastrophe. He wanted something to happen, but also to bear witness to the pantomime and not be the clown, whom the joke is on. Tathastu. He bore witness.

To an event that would cause his life to fall, like your new phone slipping from your hands and time is slowed like Kolkatas's trams which otherwise, is a city as busy as a bee. You are completely aware of what is happening and the repercussions of it, but you can't move a muscle. Time has tied your hands, legs, senses and your thoughts. All you can do is bear witness.

The same unfolded on that day but the only difference was that there was no couch, no floor, no pit, no well, no seabed, no trench, no chasm to catch the god forsaken phone.

It was sundown, when Gautham and his parents descended down the stairs to go to the hospital to see Paapa. She was in the casualty ward which was at floor -1. Gautham wondered what -1 was. He felt irritated that he couldn't remember. Then he comforted himself with the thought that they would teach integers in 6th grade again. As they walked in, he saw Paapa. Both her legs were raised and suspended in the air with a stand. Her head was oddly lower than her torso. She looked like a slanting line, Gautham thought. He wanted to laugh, but controlled it, sensing his mother might give him *the* look. There was another boy by the bed, whom Gautham had never before seen in his life.

"Where are your parents? Is this how you ride a bicycle?" threatened Gautham's dad. He had never heard this voice of his father. Not even when Gautham had broken the neighbor's bike headlight, while playing cricket. The remaining part of that memory was foggy. Perhaps because he wanted to forget the single most important incident that damaged his life beyond repair.

Paapa was apparently in a cycle accident. She was on the road and a cycle was on it too. India's unity in diversity couldn't accommodate lorries, MTC buses, cars, bikes, cycles and Paapa on the same road. His Paapa's hips were broken. So was his family now. Two daughters of Paapa, caught in the wrong world, didn't or couldn't take care of her. What happened next was what usually happens in a stalemate. Negotiations. They tried to sort out who would do what. Like two stateswomen ceding and conquering territories. Unfortunately, like in some of the epics, the advisor is always evil. Guided by bad counsel, the two decided never to see each other again. But who would see Paapa then, nobody spoke about.

Ninth grade came as a relief for Gautham, or so he thought. One random day, he decided he should confess his feelings to the girl he liked (crush meant something else then). Her parents called her something else, but to Gautham, she was his betrayer. Tamil cinema and it's lyricists taught him so. Although he never really played a role in her life, he firmly believed she was the cause of his pain.

"Enough is enough, either you tell her or I will" said the flat catalyst friend who waited 7 lives to say his line. But how? 90's tamil film directors to the rescue again . A love letter. He wrote a terrible love poem and gave it to her. What he expected were only two options, one she tears it and throws it in his face and two she is too shocked by his gesture and breaks into tears. What happened was not on the storyboard.

She giggled, blushed, looked at him for a good 5 seconds and said yes. The earth rotates at 1,670 km/hour at the equator. For Gautham alone it was brought to a sudden halt. He had thought up hundreds of possibilities, in one of which he even got suspended from school but there was not even a frame where he saw the girl blush. Now taken aback by this unexpected peripeteia, he broke into tears.

The girl was too shocked by this and decided to flee. There were about 11 people around him and he cried for more than a quarter of an hour like an infant newly pushed into this unholy globe. Schools eat incidents like these for breakfast. The bullies pounced on him like Rahul Dravid does at first slip. There was no redemption for his sin for it was too grave. His father was not poor, but not rich enough to change schools mid-academic year. The next 4 years in his high school were longer than all of Ashwathamma's years on Earth put together.

Twelfth Board Exams arrived for Gautham on a Bolero that said G in red and bold on the number plate. Gautham was more relieved than scared to be honest. For he was glad that his high school was almost over and now he could proceed to college with several brave puranas that never really happened, which he would slowly inject to his new friends and prayed that none of his schoolmates joined the same course. Although he was done with school, his school wasn't done with him. PGT teachers with personal problems and no concept of therapy take it out in two ways. Earlier it was physical abuse of the students, but now it is just gaslighting the students about the board exams and instilling maximum fear in them. It was a recompense for the trauma caused by their dysfunctional families.

Gautham too had these kinds of teachers. The yield of the teachers' therapy session was sweaty, timid and frightened students, who, was it not for their artificially inseminated fear, would ace these exams. There were no students on the schoolyard that day only cattle in line before the slaughterhouse.

A sheep called Gautham was the most afraid. Once the cattle finished praying, they were assorted into chambers according to their ear tag numbers. Gautham trotted to his chamber, where 35 other sheep were already present. His train of thought had derailed at Balasore and the relief train at Kavaraipettai. No help was coming.

In this state of affairs, he received the answer booklet and filled out all his details, snout mark, hoof size, yarn yield. By the time he finished filling it out his sweaty hoofs had smudged the ink of the previous credentials. Horror. Aristotle smiled down upon him. Gautham tried to do a recon and calm down. Most sensibly, he tried to erase the smudged ink. The booklet's first page tore off in his hand making a huge noise. He could've just apologized and gotten a new one.There was one big little issue, their ear tag numbers were printed on the papers.

The dude who was incharge of that particular center was particularly strict. He was a noble man, a math teacher who believed in setting examples. Is that why he only taught them the example sums and always assigned the exercise problems for homework? One could assume so. He set an example out of Gautham too. He announced the tragedy that had taken place, the causal agent of the said tragedy and called him on stage in front of 400 sheep. Gautham stood there, head down, and a small teardrop rolled down from his eye to his chin through his cheek. Gautham never really lifted his head after that.

Reader, you must think that though these instances may be sad or even pitiable, it could happen to everyone. There wasn't a significant role that was played by Paapa's incident. Gautham's sentence was not death, it was something that made him prefer death over life once every 3 years. Just before Gautham graduated Paapa left Gautham. Forever.

He was prohibited from visiting her since the accident, but his mother now ensured he attended her funeral. Indian funerals are more like IPOs. More people are interested in who gets what, than the number of people who actually feel the loss. They fought for who gets the gold and who gets the property. Gautham got her love. Nobody wanted a fight over that. He didn't mind the fighting or the rawness of human instinct that oozed out of the adults. He sat there, his back rested on the wall, his eyes rested on her carcass, his heart rested on her soul. Paapa seemed to say, Good riddance more than goodbye. She was pleased to see her offsprings who abandoned her fight over her belongings. She wished more than anything in all the worlds to laugh out the loudest, meanest laugh she could salvage and bless them for one last time that their inheritance would be the end of them.

It was.

Gautham's mother was less fit for this planet, so the fitter sister survived. She got most of the inheritance while Gautham's father sulked in debt, like a teenager who sulks in vanity. Both the daughters of despair were doomed then on. Their own mother's blessing caught on to them like a polythene cover that sucks up to a motorcycle wheel that is clearly committed. The wheel might not want the cover, but the cover doesn't give a hoot about it.

In the year of our lord, two thousand and twenty four, Gautham was still miserable. But now he had a cycle of his own to be miserable with. An old one that reminded him of postmen. Do postmen despise emails or do they also give out their own ones for coupons at the bill counters of clothing stores. Just as he was drooling upon the clothing store bill counters, paapa came from nowhere to the middle of the road. By the time Gautham could come back from the bill counters, it had already happened. He ran over her. She fell and so did he. 4 or 5 people who were nowhere to be found just an instant ago crowded the place. They tried to help paapa up, but she was in too much pain so she shrieked. That shriek pierced Gautham's heart like a shard of glass.

He stood there at the roadside and stared into nothing as the passers-by unaware of what they were doing accused him of hitting the old lady.

Gautham thought about this paapa's gautham for a while. He lifted his head up to see an oncoming lorry and he closed his eyes again with an exhale.

finis.

VII

A CHRISTMAS CAROL

'Twas a cold morning of January in Chennai. The weather wasn't the only one that was cold to the people. It was time itself, too haughty to slow down like the horse from that Sangam poem. In the said poem, the maiden is anxiously waiting to catch a glimpse of her lover, if you can call him that, after you have suspended the sensibilities of this century for art's sake. The war horse that seems to intentionally one-up the girl, treads rapidly past her door. She cries out in pain to the horse and pleads him to not go so fast as he is used to in the battlements, for she pledges the world to extend the short glimpse of her lover by a few instants. The people of Chennai plead time only once in a year. This time period ranges anywhere from the middle-aged December to a post mid-life crisis January. Time, unsurprisingly, has more conceit than the horse, so it doesn't even care to read the wish-letters of the holy people of this unholy land.

The only time they could put off most things until after the harvest festival or hurry to win a race against Virgin Mary. Mother Mary always wins. There was only one person who managed to equal Mother Mary's time, the non-Virgin Yashodha who rid herself of the parasite that was in her womb for the past 40 weeks. The unorthodox, non-westernized couple, Yashodha and Gopal, the parents of the parasite didn't mind paying a tribute to time, by naming it after the day it was born, Christmas.

14 such tributes to time, 14 such heartfelt proposals to the horse and to time, and 14 such cold rejections later, Christy turned fourteen. She loves these days as lovingly as a loyal Chennaiite does, solely because you get parole from the kind, fertile stepmother, to run back breathlessly to your own mother, barren; but still your mother. If she could yield, her children wouldn't have to leave her again to go back to their stepmothers. But she can't, naturally because of their father.

Christy didn't have a stepmother, so she always went to her Athai's, for this short era of joy and kindness. It was always on the local train that she was taken to her aunt's house. An apt moniker for what was supposed to be called the suburban or the EMUs, though nobody called it that.

The local trains save for this short interval functioned completely differently. There were modern Macbeths that not just skipped a step while ascending but also while descending. That fraction of the moment they were suspended completely in air, gave them the libido, the city had robbed them of. There was someone, who was always late, or even if they weren't they ran. They rushed. Hustled. Skimmed past the crowd. At least here they weren't at the back of the race as usual. At least here, they could tell themselves that they had won something. Not of value or permanence but of transience, for that short while, they could lie to themselves that all this hustling and bustling and rushing and out-of-breathing was not for nothing. Was not just to buy random stuff that bloated bloatocrats further. This win was theirs alone, aided by foolish youth that just ticks away at their health, patiently, almost as patiently as the cow-gods outside the shrines of the Destroyer.

Christy has seen this pantomime, one too many times. The 20/20 salesmen, the women who aren't women enough for society, so they have to clap for themselves, because nobody else will, the abandoned parents of the doomed children who walk around, not seeking alms, just children, the 20/20 reps, who play songs from a speaker that try to be Carols but aren't or some Emersons among those reps, who play their own music, the intact-limbed prohibitionists, who seek funds from their wives for their campaign against the liquid-Satan, the wonderfully open-throated fruit engineers, against whom opera singers don't stand a chance, the rhetoricians propagating their products. But these were just the producers. The consumers are aplenty.

The middle-aged men, who think they are sacrificing their lives for their families, but are really just doing it because they have no other choice and love telling Were-it-not-for-me stories, when they are out of things to sacrifice; the ones who sacrifice everything they have and even what they don't but are blinded by too much love to see it; the previously abused children who have to howl and swear and hoot and perform dangerous tricks, just so that they aren't abused further; those that wear spectacles which expired eons ago but aren't willing to change them, and subsequently and vehemently claim, roses are blue; the major rest that are caught in the spiral of algorithms, periodically confirming their fall with their own thumbs, the sleepers, the dreamers, the orchestra and finally the watchers, who are just in the trains, doing nothing else but watching, patiently with the surety of time watching the apocalypse.

Christy is a simple girl. Her days are even more so. The peak hour morning 8.15 ladies special to the Trident station, to school, to her place in her class, to her place in her tuition which really doesn't teach her anything but gives time for her Yashodha to complete her shift, to take her back on the evening 7.50 back to her place at home. Nowhere else but her place where she rightfully belonged. Whose right? Christy didn't know. Christy's world was the real economically weaker, poorer section of society. Which really just meant, they were so poor that they didn't get a chance to be green of others, simply because they didn't know green symbolised jealousy. Perhaps that was why the wormhole that appears to the fag end of the dying year, gives them some kind of relief, or so they believe. For they didn't know Nietzsche too.

Every 6th of the new month, her mother was paid. Every 6th, Christy got a parotta (a flatbread) Not a set, not with the saalna (the gravy); just one parotta. That was burnt because Yashodha paid 8 rupees; the burn was a privilege even the ones who gave the full 15 rupees weren't entitled to. Christy couldn't have anything to go with the parotta, because only then could Gopal afford something to go with his liquid-Satan. Christy would console Yashodha, saying she at least has the Trident hillock for her to dip the parotta in.

The hillock was not just there for Christy's parotta, for it was older than parotta itself. But for Christy it was her Saalna. It was caved in the middle. It was so weirdly caved that it looked like the old sofa at Christy's Athais place. When Christy was younger than now, Yashodha told her that it was the throne of an early God. The "scandalous rascal" that made us, as Yashodha called him. The hill was difficult to find on her happy days but impossible to unsee on the sad ones. They were always there. Yashodha, the trident hillock, and Christy's ball of yarn which she has held onto ever since the first time her uniform tore.

Just there, everyday. It was a chair that also, contradictorily, sat on a couch the whole day. Pretty much like the watcher on the local train, on whom time and space imprint themselves on. Permanently. Doing nothing. Saying nothing. Hearing everything. Pretty much like every middle class Indian who witnesses a social evil unfolding before their eyes, but just shuts up and trots on. Because they couldn't afford another revolution.

On that cold, January day of the 14th rejection, Christy and Yashodha were returning from her aunt's place. Back to where they belonged. "Wait, what if we took the metro for once?" demanded Christy to make the most out of this wormhole before returning to their own mother who was kind to all but them. Yashoda dismissed the thought like an obvious logical fallacy. "We don't have money for that and you know it !" said Yashodha.

"We do ! And you know it too.", the unfamiliar teen rebelliousness answered for Christy. She was as taken aback as Yashodha was.

" Athai gave **me** 50 rupees! I get to decide what has to be done with that money, not you, not Gopal" Christy found herself continuing and unable to stop. She didn't want to.

This newfound individualism, as recent as Australia, caught Yashoda's tongue like a feline. Unable to quote the scriptures or to make up an obscure superstition, Yashodha fell silent. Fell deeply silent.

Mounam sammadhaṃ.This was the first time where silence means consent for the good.

Nobody could stop Christy now. " Please ma, for the next two months I don't want the parotta, so now we have 16 rupees more. It's 32 rupees for each of us and we could get down at the Trident station. And carry on like it never happened."

Yashodha wanted to teach her daughter that that's not how money works. But she felt she had something more important to learn. So it did happen.

They got their fancy QR coded tickets, scanned it through et voila. It was crazy how 32 rupees took them somewhere lightyears beyond the local trains.

The voice of the announcer. It sounded like her Athai (aunt). Sweet, welcoming and in no rush for the first time in her life. Unlike the local train announcer, who reminded them of Gopal's dead mother. The reassuring thought of her death compensated for the incredible fear in Yashodha.

January was not as cruel as May, but the metro was no match. It wasn't too cold. Or too suffocating. It was just right, like the almost-a-kiss, Yashodha plants on Christy after the loud-thud-no-scream-cheek-bruise nights with Gopal.

The consumers were completely different on the metros and to both Yashoda and Christy's abrupt shock, there were no producers. They could do without that.

The metro ride was nothing short of the roller-coaster rides on the amusement park commercials Christy was addicted to in the railway station televisions. She never thought she would get to ride one, but she was. Thanks to her thirty two rupees.

Yashodha was suddenly caught by her wrist with the thought of Gopal's reminder for Athai's money. Well, Satan could do without Gopal for one night.

Somewhere in the middle, a church choir caroling, got on the train and shortly after burst into the most spirited Christmas song Christy had ever heard. She was half-annoyed and half-amazed, when she turned to look at Yashodha. To her surprise

Yashodha was muttering the lyrics of the song. This time there were no ghosts to help them, but they were just fine by themselves.

There was only one thing missing though, “the Trident hillock.” reminded Yashodha. “He couldn’t come with us.”

Christy smirked and looked at Yashodha dead in the eye when she said,

“Why would he move now, after all this time ?”

finis.

VIII

AND THEN, THERE WILL BE NONE

And they lived happily ever after, on a normal day in Sep... Oh wait! Our months of the year aren't applicable to them. For it wasn't going to be until another 3500 years until Pope Gregory XIII would be so kind as to structuralise time for us and leave it to the hardworking colonial Europeans to spread the word. So,

twas a normal day with a climate unusual to us in Mohenjo Daro. Since our country's culture, if I can dare say so because the former is an infant (77 years) when put on equal terms with the latter, bids me to give you some context; I shall oblige.

Dear reader,

Have you ever felt good for a little too long, that you start to feel this uneasy chisel in your mind, in anticipation of something bad to happen? This, verbatim was what was on the minds of the people of Mohenjo Daro or at least the Citadel half of them.

"Enough is enough Amma. We will not tolerate everything the Elders do just because they were born in the Citadel and we weren't", pronounced Daughter, as she stormed out of the room. On hearing this Abba rushed in from the kitchen trying to stop Daughter, but Amma declared sternly, "Get back to the kitchen. Just because Daughter has decided to break a holy custom doesn't mean you get a free pass into the living room does it? We cannot commit blasphemy twice to Agni on the same day can we?

Make sure you and Son get supper ready. A table for 1 will do I guess. I am going to the Bath to witness the ritual. I'll be back in time for supper" declared Amma.

"As you wish Amma" supplicated Abba before her.

Keezh Mohenjo Daro or the home of the commons was feeling rather rebellious that day. Like an Indian teen with no concept of individualism suddenly feels, when exposed to their counterparts from the West. Daughter with her equals was going to pull off something terrible. Something beautiful. Something terribly beautiful. The first coup in human history.

Little did they know that if time was non-linear, which I hope it is, anyone in the place of Daughter and her equals would have done the same thing.

Agni had begun to sink downwards for his sleep. This signified nothing extraordinary except for the fact that before he woke up, the Elders wouldn't be there to welcome him as usual. This also signified the beginning of the ritual.

The Ritual; it was as spectacular as a director's producer-destroying description of a set he wants to build for nothing more than a dance number. The bath was freshly filled with water from the Indus. The Elders Superior and the Elders Inferior had adorned their ceremonial robes and were descending steps of it. Fire torches surrounded the Bath, accompanying their holders. The entire female population of Mohenjo Daro was assembled at the Bath.

So was Amma and so was Daughter. The equals were evenly spread out among the Citadel people, concealing their weapons. The only public display of religion that takes place in the city, was their target day. They wanted to strike the heart of their beliefs. Something much like Darwin, but only eons before.

The Superior Elders descended to the last step where the water didn't dare to rise, and stopped. One Elder, the Eldest, with the help of the adjacent Elders stooped with difficulty and touched her head to the water. At this exact moment all the Mohenjo Daroites started humming and beating their chest like a tomtom. This carried on for a minute or so until one of the adjacent Elders rose to the platform and declared " As there are no other nominations or oppositions to the incumbent Eldest will now continue as Eldest for the ..."

"I oppose" shouted Daughter at the top of her lungs. The sound of objects, people, their organs, their tissues, their cells, their atoms coming to a rest was deafening. She had spoken. An inferior had spoken. Spivak smiled from above (remember, time is non-linear).

"Blasphemy! Blasphemy!" cried one of the adjacent Elders. "Hang that " shouted a Citadel commoner. No sooner had she completed, than one of Daughter's equals shouted "I oppose". After that the rest of the equals joined in one by one without missing a beat. There was a much expected uproar from the crowd, while Amma cringed and tried to hide herself in the midst of the crowd. The incumbent Eldest raised up her hand and the people had started to fall silent until the last person in the crowd had seen Eldest's palm in the air. "Well my dear, what exactly do you oppose?" asked the Eldest with the apt nonchalance of a leader.

To this all the equals and daughter looked at each other as though they had rehearsed it, and started humming and beating their chest. They performed this for a good minute until they all stopped at exactly the same moment. And raised up their hand in the air and yelled "The Citadel, Your Ritual, Your Custom, Your Agni (to this there was a gasp louder than before from the crowd) and above all, You"

The Eldest was not surprised. The bull didn't get her tongue. She thought to herself, addressing Daughter "You're late".

Now she proclaimed "Seize them and take them away, they shall be sacrificed at the next festival!" To this there were murmurs among the crowd. Seeds of discontent were visibly sprouting and the Eldest made no mistake and squashed it with her imaginary

Guccis. "Agni demands it". This would suffice for now as the crowd went silent again.

Thus began the fall. The fall of the people of the Indus. Little did they know, that thousands of years later, there would be people that would look at them in awe, how once, long ago life thrived here. Once upon a time.

finis.

www.ingramcontent.com/pod-product-compliance
Lightning Source LLC
LaVergne TN
LVHW090131160826
845673LV00017B/1945

* 9 7 9 8 8 9 7 2 4 1 2 5 5 *